D0564086

rhcbooks.com

ISBN 978-0-7364-4072-1 (hardcover)
ISBN 978-0-7364-4073-8 (paperback)

Printed in the United States of America

10 9 8 7 6 5 4 3 2 1

DISNEY · PIXAR

SOUL

The Deluxe Junior Novelization

Adapted by Tenny Nellson

Random House 🏠 **New York**

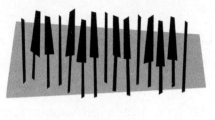

One

Joe Gardner was not someone who made people sit up and take notice. Not at first, anyway. He was tall but mild-mannered, with a thin mustache and a timid smile. He wore glasses with heavy black frames. At forty-six, his black hair was just starting to turn gray. He didn't care about clothes, so his wardrobe consisted mostly of slacks and black turtlenecks.

Anyone meeting Joe for the first time would never guess that within his chest, his heart beat with white-hot passion—a fire that burned for just one thing.

Joe *loved* jazz music.

He'd fallen for jazz when he was twelve years old. Since that day, he'd devoted his life to the music— listening to it, studying it, playing it. Jazz was the first thing he thought of in the morning. At night, he went to sleep with riffs and codas swirling through his brain.

For Joe, the incredible thing about jazz music, the thing that kept it from getting old, was that there were so many ways to play it. And all those ways made you feel something different.

Jazz could be bold and confident. Or playful. Or melancholic. Some jazz made you feel on top of the world. And when you were down in the dumps, jazz could be a balm for your soul.

And then there was the kind of jazz that made you feel like you were being run over by a garbage truck. In other words, jazz played by a middle-school band.

Unfortunately, Joe was deeply familiar with this variety.

On a Friday morning in late fall, Joe stood at the podium in the M.S. 74 band room. Armed with only a conductor's baton, he bravely tried to coax a harmony from the noise assaulting his ears.

"One, two, three, four! Stay on the beat! Two, three, four—" Joe shouted, waving the baton in vain. He could barely make himself heard over the honking and shrieking of the horn section. "That's a C-sharp, horns!"

CRASH! A trombonist knocked over her music stand. The trumpeter next to her was slouched so far down that he appeared to be playing into his navel. One of the saxophonists seemed to be playing the wrong song entirely—probably because the kid was paying more attention to his cell phone than the sheet music.

Joe turned to Connie, a petite trombonist in the first row. She was his last hope. "All you, Connie. Go for it!"

Connie raised her trombone to her lips and began her solo. The notes rang out clear and strong over the cacophony. She closed her eyes, swaying as she played.

Joe smiled. Once in a blue moon, a student came along who made teaching almost seem worth it. Connie was one of those students. The kid was *good*.

But then the other kids started to laugh. Joe heard their snickers ricocheting around the room.

Connie heard them, too. She seemed to wilt in her chair. Her notes faltered.

"Hang on, hang on!" Joe hollered. He tapped the music stand with his baton. With a few honks and squeaks, the music ground to a halt.

"What are y'all laughing at?" Joe asked sternly.

The students gave him blank looks.

"So Connie got lost in it. That's a *good* thing." Joe walked over to the piano. Still talking, he began to play. "I remember one time, my dad took me to this jazz club. It was the last place I wanted to be. But then I see this guy playing piano. . . ." Joe ran his hands over the keys, riffing. "It's like he's singing. And I swear, the next thing I know, it's like he floats off the stage. That guy was lost in the music. He was in it—and he took us with him. I wanted to learn how to talk like that. That's when I knew I was born to play."

He ended with a flourish, then turned to look at his students. "Connie knows what I mean. Right, Connie?"

Connie shrank in her seat. She looked like she wanted to disappear. "I'm twelve," she said.

A knock at the classroom door interrupted the moment. "I'll be right back. Practice your scales," Joe told the class.

He stepped out into the hall. Ms. Arroyo, the school vice principal, was standing there. "Sorry to interrupt, Mr. Gardner," she said. "I wanted to deliver the good news personally." She handed Joe a letter.

Joe opened it and scanned the contents. With a shock, he realized it was a full-time job offer—his first ever.

"No more part-time for you," the vice principal said, beaming. "They finally cleared enough in the budget. You're now our full-time band teacher! Job security. Medical benefits. Pension." She looked at Joe expectantly.

"Wow. That's . . . great," Joe managed.

Vice Principal Arroyo held out a hand for Joe to shake. "Welcome to the M.S. 74 family, Joe. Permanently."

Joe forced himself to smile.

Permanently. The word echoed in Joe's mind for the rest of the morning. He knew he should be happy. He'd barely been scraping by on his part-time salary. This job would change all that.

But his position at M.S. 74 was only supposed to be temporary, just something to keep him afloat until he got his big break. The only thing Joe wanted was to play great music—and not just for a bunch of half-awake middle schoolers.

When class let out that day, Joe still felt uncertain. He decided to go see his mother. Maybe she would have some words of advice. Not to mention that he had laundry to do.

Libba Gardner owned a small tailoring shop in Queens, New York. She was a tall, elegant woman in her sixties with cropped white hair and a no-nonsense attitude. As Joe folded his laundry, he filled her in on the job offer.

"After all these years, my prayers have been answered! A full-time job!" she said, clasping her hands together.

"Yeah," Joe said heavily.

His mother fixed him with a stern look. "You're going to tell them yes, right?"

"Don't worry, Mom," Joe said. "I've got a plan."

Libba's lips pursed like she'd sucked on a lemon. "You've always got a plan. Maybe you need to have a backup plan, too, for when your plan falls through."

Joe didn't know why he felt so stunned. She'd never supported his career choices. Why had he thought this time would be any different?

Libba sighed. "Joey," she said in a softer voice, "we

didn't struggle giving you an education just so you could be a middle-aged man washing your underwear in my shop."

"Yeah. But, Mom—" Joe began.

Libba cut him off. "With this job, you'll finally be able to put that dead-end gigging behind you."

"Yeah, but . . ."

"And just think," Libba went on, "playing music will finally be your real career. So you're going to tell them yes, right?"

Joe opened his mouth to protest. Then he closed it. He knew nothing he could say would change his mother's mind.

And maybe she was right. Maybe this job really was the best career he could hope for.

Joe let out a long sigh. Then he nodded. "Yeah."

"Good." Libba looked satisfied.

Bzzzz. Joe's phone vibrated in his pocket. He pulled it out and saw an unfamiliar number. "Hello?"

"How you been, Mr. G?" said a voice Joe recognized but couldn't place. "It's Curley—uh, Lamont. Lamont Baker."

"Curley!" Joe was surprised to hear from his former student. It had been—what? At least a decade since

Curley had graduated from middle school. "Hey, man. How you been?"

"Great, Mr. Gardner."

Joe chuckled. "You can call me Joe now. I'm not your teacher anymore."

"Okay, Mr. Gardner. Hey, look," Curley said, getting to the point, "I'm the new drummer in the Dorothea Williams Quartet, and we're kicking off our tour with a show at The Half Note tonight. . . ."

"Dorothea Williams?" Joe yelped. "You're kidding. Congratulations, man! Wow. I would die a happy man if I could perform with Dorothea Williams."

"Well," Curley replied, "this could be your lucky day. . . ."

Moments later, Joe hung up the phone, his heart pounding. *Dorothea Williams! I'm gonna try out for the Dorothea Williams!*

Dorothea Williams was one of the greatest living saxophone players, a queen of the New York jazz scene. The chance to play with a musician like her only came around once in a lifetime.

Joe made a quick excuse to Libba and dashed for the

door. He headed for the subway that would take him to the West Village, where The Half Note was located.

Twenty minutes later, Joe sprinted up to a green brick building with a red awning over the doorway. Once inside, he paused to catch his breath. His eyes swept over the black-and-white photographs lining the stairwell that led down to the club. All of Joe's heroes were there: Duke Ellington. John Coltrane. Miles Davis. Ella Fitzgerald. Thelonius Monk. Ornette Coleman. Dizzy Gillespie. Charlie Parker. Bill Evans. And so many more.

And now it was Joe's turn. At least, he hoped so.

"There he is! My man!" Curley was waiting for Joe at the bottom of the stairs. He was taller and broader than the last time Joe had seen him, and his head was shaved bald. But he had the same sweet, round face he'd had at thirteen.

"Hey, Curley," Joe said, shaking his hand.

"Leon skipping town really put us in a bind, man," Curley told him.

"I'll bet." Joe tried to look sympathetic. But inwardly, he thanked his lucky stars. If he ever met Leon, he was going to take him out to dinner for giving him this chance!

"I'm glad you made it," Curley said, leading Joe into the club.

As Joe's eyes adjusted to the semidarkness, he saw Dorothea onstage, warming up on her sax. Silhouetted against the red curtain, she looked as regal as a queen on her throne. But it was the music that stopped Joe in his tracks. The sound coming from her sax was warm and rich enough to drink. He stood there for a moment, dazzled.

"Hey, Dorothea," said Curley, "this is the cat I was telling you about. My old middle-school band teacher, Mr. Gardner!"

"Call me Joe, Dorothea . . . I mean, um, Ms. Williams. It's a pleasure. Wow. This is amazing," Joe gushed.

Dorothea lowered her saxophone. She gave Joe a long, appraising look. The silence stretched on awkwardly.

To fill it, Curley added, "Joe is Ray Gardner's son."

"So," Dorothea said at last. "We're down to middle-school band teachers now."

Joe glanced helplessly at Curley. Did that mean he was out? Before he'd even played?

"Get on up here, Teach," Dorothea commanded, rising from her chair. "We ain't got all day."

Joe sprang onto the stage. He barely had time to take a seat at the piano when Dorothea snapped her fingers.

"What . . . what are we playing?" Joe asked.

In answer, Dorothea started to play. Curley and the bassist, Miho, a slender woman with a fedora tipped over one eye, joined in without missing a beat.

Joe played a few chords, trying to keep up and figure out where they were going. After a few bars he caught on and pressed the keys harder. Dorothea turned to him and raised an eyebrow, as if to say, *It's all you. Show me what you got.*

Joe took a deep breath. He closed his eyes and began his solo. The Half Note, Dorothea, and Curley all faded into the background. It was just Joe and the piano. He felt like he was floating—floating on a sea of music. . . .

At some point, Joe realized that the room had gone silent. He opened his eyes. Dorothea, Curley, and Miho were all staring at him.

"Uh, sorry." Joe lifted his hands from the keyboard,

feeling his face go hot. "I zoned out a little back there."

"Joe Gardner," Dorothea said. "Where have you been?"

"I've been teaching middle-school band," he answered. "But on weekends, I—"

"You got a suit?" Dorothea interrupted. When Joe hesitated, she commanded, "Get a suit, Teach. A good suit. Back here tonight. First show's at nine. Sound check's at seven. We'll see how you do."

Joe grinned. But his insides were doing cartwheels. He'd done it! He was the new pianist for the Dorothea Williams Quartet!

Two

"YEAH! WOO-HOO!" Joe burst from The Half Note, punching a fist in the air. "You see that, Dad?" Joe called up to the heavens. "That's what I'm talking about!"

A man pushing a stroller walked past. "Look up!" Joe cried, pointing at the club's marquee. "You know what that's gonna say? 'Joe Gardner'!"

The man eyed him like he was a lunatic, but Joe didn't care. He took off down the street, swiping madly on his cell phone. He had to tell everyone about his gig—the one he'd been waiting for all his life.

Well, almost *everyone,* Joe thought. There was no need to mention it to Libba, not yet. He wanted to enjoy this moment just a bit longer without getting an earful from his mother.

"You're never gonna believe what happened! I got the gig!" he exclaimed to a friend on his phone. Joe was so caught up in his excitement that he didn't notice he was walking through a construction site.

Crash! A stack of bricks tumbled down, missing Joe by inches.

"Hey, pal!" a construction worker shouted at him. "You're gonna get hurt!"

But Joe didn't hear. Still talking on the phone, he stepped out into traffic.

Vroom! A bus roared past so close, it nearly swept his hat off his head. Joe walked on, oblivious.

"Forget class," he yammered into his phone. "I'm in a different class. I'm in a Dorothea Williams class, buddy. You know what I'm saying?"

Joe turned a corner and nearly collided with an angry dog coming toward him. The dog lunged at him, barking and snarling, while its owner tugged at its leash to restrain it.

"Whoops, sorry!" Joe said, dodging the dog's teeth. He spun on his heel, backing into the street—right into the path of an oncoming motorcycle. The motorcyclist swerved to avoid him. It was so close, Joe's hat was nearly knocked off again!

Finally, Joe came to his senses. He was standing in the middle of the street, in New York City!

He began to hurry toward the safety of the sidewalk. But he'd taken only a step—when his foot fell onto nothing. He had walked right over an uncovered manhole.

Joe screamed as he plunged into darkness.

"Oof!" Joe grunted when he landed. He sat up gingerly, but he didn't feel any pain. *Well, this is good,* he thought. *At least I didn't break anything.*

Joe blinked, trying to see. The blackness was absolute—the kind of darkness where you couldn't even see your fingers in front of your face.

But . . . it was weird. Joe *could* see his hand. It looked like it was softly glowing. Slowly, he got to his feet. As he did, he became aware that he was standing on some kind of moving sidewalk—a *slide*walk.

"Hello?" he called into the darkness. "Hello?" His voice seemed strangely small. Up ahead, Joe saw a glimmer of light. The gleam sharpened into a large white circle, and he was headed right toward it.

"What the—?"

Joe had a bad feeling about that light. He turned and began to walk the other way, but the slidewalk continued to carry him forward. All Joe managed to do was walk in place.

He glanced over his shoulder. The great white light loomed, humming faintly. And despite his efforts, it looked even bigger than before. Joe started to run. There had to be some way out!

"Oh!" he said. In the distance, heading toward the light, he spotted three figures on the walkway. Joe ran toward them. As he got closer, he saw they were a young woman, an elderly man, and a woman who appeared to be older than the man. Like Joe, they were glowing softly.

"What's your name?" asked the older woman.

"I'm Joe. Joe Gardner," he replied. "Look, I'm not supposed to be here."

"It must have been sudden for you," said the older woman. "See, I'm one hundred and six years old, honey. Been waiting a long time for this."

"For what?" Joe asked, confused.

She pointed ahead of her. "The Great Beyond."

"The Great Beyond?" Joe's uneasy feeling sharpened into panic. "As in . . . beyond *life*?"

"Yeah," the man said.

"Exciting, isn't it?" the older woman said, smiling.

"No!" Joe cried, backing away from them. "No, no, no, no! Listen, I have a gig tonight. I can't die now!"

"I really don't think you have a lot of say about this," the man pointed out.

"Yes, I do!" Joe exclaimed. "I'm not dying the *very* day I got my shot. I'm due! Heck, I'm *over*due. Nuh-uh! I'm outta here."

He spun on his heel and once again started to run against the flow of the moving sidewalk.

"I don't think you're supposed to go that way," the older woman called after him.

Joe didn't care. "This can't happen," he told himself. "I'm *not* dying today. Not when my life has just started!"

He glanced back. Behind him, the slidewalk had begun to ascend like an escalator, carrying the three souls upward toward The Great Beyond.

Fzzzt! With an electric crackle, they disappeared into the light.

"Gahhh!" Joe screamed, running faster. "I'm not finished! I GOTTA GET BACK! I DON'T WANT TO DIE!"

As he scrambled against the slidewalk, he saw more souls coming toward him.

"Run!" Joe screamed at a soul who looked like a sad-eyed young man. "Why aren't you running? Don't you want to live?"

"I dunno." The soul shrugged disinterestedly, and the slidewalk carried him away.

Joe ran on, passing more and more souls. They appeared to be all ages and spoke many different languages. Some seemed freaked out, while others seemed at peace. Most just looked confused.

Joe pushed past all of them, searching for an exit. "Help, I'm not done!" he panted. "I've got to get back!"

Joe tripped and tumbled off the edge of the slidewalk. He fell against an invisible barrier. It stretched beneath his weight, and then ripped. Joe found himself falling . . .

and falling . . .

and falling. . . .

Three

Joe opened his eyes. He was lying in a landscape of rolling blue-green hills. Not far away, he could see a cluster of bizarre buildings that were made of some kind of gossamer material. They appeared to be crafted from air and light.

Suddenly, Joe was surrounded by small souls. They poked at him curiously like a group of unruly children.

"Now, now," said a calm voice above them. "Let's give the mentor some room."

Joe raised his eyes, and he found himself looking up at the strangest person he had ever seen—though he doubted that "person" was the right word. She was tall as a tree and looked as if she had been drawn with one continuous line, or twisted from a single piece of wire. She didn't really look like a human being—more like a doodle of one.

With the tolerant manner of a camp counselor, she herded the rowdy group of fuzzy little beings away from Joe. "Sorry," she told him. "New souls."

"Is this heaven?" Joe asked.

"It's easy to get turned around," the counselor told Joe. "This isn't The Great Beyond. It's The Great Before!"

"The Great Before?" Joe repeated, feeling more confused than ever.

"You must be lost," the counselor said. "I'll get you back to the group."

Without warning, the counselor suddenly changed shape, becoming a large, strange beast that also appeared to be a bus.

"Come on, little souls!" the counselor said. The new souls climbed aboard. Not knowing what else to do, Joe followed.

The counselor immediately set off across the field, carrying them toward some buildings. "Welcome to the You Seminar!" she said. "You are in for a treat."

She stopped in front of a building that had a starburst symbol over the door. "First stop, the

Excitable Pavilion." She pointed to some new souls. "You four. In you go!"

The new souls entered the building. Seconds later, they emerged from the other side, bouncing like kids on pogo sticks and hollering, "Woo-hoo!"

The counselor moved on to the next building. The symbol over the door looked like a face with its nose in the air. "You five," she said, dropping off another group. "You'll be aloof."

When these new souls passed through that building, they returned with their arms folded, noses held high.

"Wait a minute," Joe said. "This is where personalities come from?"

"Of course! Do you think people are just born with them?" The counselor smiled, as if the idea amused her.

"So how do they get to Earth, then?" Joe asked.

"They use the Earth Portal . . . ," the counselor replied.

Ahead, Joe saw a number of hazy rings that formed a sort of platform. Through the hole in the middle, Joe could see Planet Earth far below. New souls crowded around the hole. Cheered on by counselors, they were leaping off the platform like swimmers, diving toward the blue-green planet.

Earth! Joe thought. It was right there!

"Once they get a complete personality, of course," the counselor added. She turned to glance at Joe. But he was gone.

At the edge of the Earth Portal, Joe squeezed through the crowd of new souls. He plunged off the edge and found himself free-falling through space, surrounded by new souls.

"Woooooo-hoooo!" Joe cried as he plummeted toward Earth.

Wham! Joe struck another invisible barrier and bounced off. As the other souls sailed on toward Earth, Joe found himself redirected and plopped back into the You Seminar.

What happened? Joe thought. He hurried back to the Earth Portal and leaped again.

He struck the barrier once more and landed back in the You Seminar. Over and over, he tried to leap to Earth, only to find himself back where he'd started.

As Joe sat, panting in frustration, the counselor passed by again. She had returned to her humanlike form.

When she saw Joe, she paused. "You sure get lost a lot." She turned and called out to another counselor, leading a different group of souls. "Hello, Jerry! Got a lost mentor for you!"

"Thanks, Jerry," the other counselor replied.

"Look," Joe said to the first counselor. "I don't think I'm supposed to be here."

"I understand," she said gently. "Mentoring isn't for everyone. You're more than welcome to opt out."

The counselor waved her hands, and a hole appeared in the atmosphere. She had opened a portal to another dimension as easily as opening a window. Through the hole, Joe could see a bright white light. The Great Beyond hummed ominously.

Joe backed away. "Actually, on second thought, the mentoring sounds like fun."

Joe grabbed a prewritten name tag from a table and followed a group of souls into a building. He had no idea what he'd just signed up for. Whatever it was, it couldn't be worse than what awaited him in The Great Beyond.

Four

Back in The Great Beyond, Terry the accountant watched the souls moving along the slidewalk. Terry was responsible for counting the souls who entered The Great Beyond. She clicked each one off on her giant abacus. Suddenly, she paused.

"That's weird," she murmured. "The count's off."

"Excuse me?" said the counselor standing next to her.

"There's a soul missing," Terry said. "The count is *off*."

"Huh." The counselor furrowed his brow in a posture of concern.

Terry frowned. "Huh" wasn't good enough. She was all about numbers. And if a soul was missing, she was going to find it.

At the Earth Portal, the You Seminar counselors were cheering their new souls on to Earth when Terry came striding up.

"Jerry," Terry barked. "We've got a problem."

The tallest counselor turned. She peered down at the squat, sharp-nosed figure. "Oh, hello there, Terry."

Skipping the pleasantries, Terry got to the point. "The count's off," she reported.

"I seriously doubt that," Jerry replied. "The count hasn't been off in centuries—"

"One hundred and fifty-one thousand souls go into The Great Beyond every day," Terry interrupted briskly. She produced an enormous abacus and began flipping the beads back and forth with practiced speed. "That's one hundred and five point two souls per minute, Jerry. One point seven five souls per second. And I count every single one of them."

"Yes, I'm aware," Jerry replied.

"It's my job to keep track of this stuff, Jerry," Terry added. "I'm the accountant."

"And we think you're doing a wonderful job," Jerry replied smoothly. "So, since accounting is *your* job, why don't *you* figure out the problem?"

"Maybe I will," Terry snapped.

"Wonderful!" the counselor exclaimed. And, as if the matter were settled, she vanished on the spot.

Terry went straight to the Hall of Everyone, where files of every soul who had ever lived or died were kept. Ignoring the cheery greeting of the counselor at the front desk, she headed for the *A* files. She yanked open the top drawer and began to flip through the files so fast, her fingers blurred.

"You're out there somewhere, little soul," Terry murmured. "And I'm gonna find you."

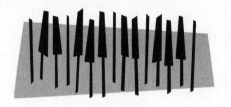

Five

In the orientation building, Joe sat in a darkened theater. Along with a handful of other souls, he watched an orientation video.

"Hello there, mentors!" exclaimed a counselor on the screen. "I'm Jerry. Here at the You Seminar, all new souls are given unique and individual personalities."

The camera cut to a series of new souls, each holding up a Personality Profile. They all had the same nondescript features and sweet, childlike voices.

"I'm an agreeable skeptic who's cautious yet flamboyant."

"I'm an irritable wallflower who's dangerously curious."

"I'm a manipulative megalomaniac who's intensely opportunistic."

"Oh, ho! This one might be a handful!" the onscreen Jerry said cheerfully. "But that's Earth's problem."

Yikes! thought Joe. *Wasn't anyone doing quality control on these souls?*

"Anyway," the counselor said lightly, "you'll notice these souls are all missing something." He pointed to the blank space on one soul's Personality Profile. "What's that last box for? Well, these souls need their 'Spark.' And that's where *you* come in!"

Joe shifted in his seat. He didn't care about Sparks. He just needed to get back to Earth!

"Maybe you'll find their Spark in the Hall of Everything, where literally anything on Earth could inspire!" Onscreen, a new soul's Personality Profile was filled in. At once, the Personality Profile transformed into an Earth Pass.

"Or perhaps," the narrator went on, "you'll prefer the Earthetarium, featuring a selection of moments from your own inspiring life! And just what provides that Spark? Well, because you've already lived, you understand. There are some things on Earth that just make life worth living!"

Joe's eyes widened. A plan was forming in his mind. Step one: Play piano for a new soul, who is so inspired that its Personality Profile instantly turns into an Earth Pass. Step two: Snatch the Earth Pass from the unsuspecting newbie and leap down to Earth in the soul's place. Step three: Wake up in his own body, play the gig with Dorothea Williams, and receive the adoration of all New York City.

"Yes!" Joe chuckled. It was foolproof!

"I know you're all excited to get to work. Good luck finding the Spark!" The video ended.

"Find the Spark!" Joe whispered to himself.

As the lights came up, another counselor stepped onto the stage. "Now it's time for my favorite part of the program," he said. "Matching you mentors with your soul mates."

A group of new souls entered through the doors at the back of the theater and made their way down to the stage.

"Our first mentor is Maria Martinez. Maria Martinez, come on down!" Jerry boomed.

There was a smattering of applause. The soul ascended the stage as highlights from her human life played on the screen behind her. Then an adorable little soul bounced onto the stage. Maria and the soul embraced, and they walked off hand in hand.

"Our next mentor," said the counselor, "is Bjorn T. Borgenson!"

There was a long pause. Joe glanced down at his nametag. *Bjorn T. Borgenson?* That was Joe!

He hurried forward. Behind the counselor, scenes from Bjorn's life were playing. On the screen, an old man spoke gently to a crying child.

Counselor Jerry exclaimed, "Dr. Borgenson is a world-renowned child psychologist who was recently awarded a Nobel Prize!"

Nobel Prize–winning doctor? thought Joe. *Hoo boy.* Oh, well. He'd be a Nobel prize–winning *walrus* if that's what it took to get his life back.

The counselor beamed. "Dr. Borgenson will be matched with soul number . . . 22."

A spotlight swooped onto the stage. But it was empty.

"Oh, we're gonna do this now?" counselor Jerry grumbled. "Excuse me." He abruptly vanished.

Joe stood there awkwardly. He could hear Jerry's voice coming from somewhere beneath the stage.

"You come out of this dimension right now!" the counselor ordered.

"How many times do I have to tell you? I don't wanna go to Earth!" another voice whined.

"Stop fighting this, 22. You *will* go to Earth and have a life!" said counselor Jerry. He reappeared on the stage holding a fuzzy green new soul, who was fighting like a wildcat.

"22 has been at the You Seminar for quite some time— *Stop it!*" the counselor hissed at the soul, who was twisting in his grip like a miniature hurricane. "She has had such notable mentors as Gandhi, Abraham Lincoln, and Mother Teresa."

"I made her cry!" the soul crowed.

"We're *truly* glad you're here, Dr. Borgenson," the counselor said to Joe, trying to hold the struggling 22 at arm's length. "It is an honor having you prepare 22 for Earth."

"I'm gonna make you wish you'd never died," 22 snarled.

"Most people wish that, 22," the counselor said wearily. He dumped the soul into Joe's arms, exclaiming, "Congratulations! Off you go!"

The moment the soul touched Joe, she melted all over him like some sort of toxic green marshmallow. As the audience clapped, the stage rotated, carrying them both away.

Six

As soon as they were out of the counselor's sight, Joe shoved 22 off him. She sprang back into her new-soul form. Like the other new souls, she glowed a soft, iridescent green. She had rosy cheeks and a cute overbite. Joe thought she was sort of adorable. Or she *would* have been adorable if she hadn't been looking at Joe like she wanted to murder him.

"Where are we?" Joe asked, looking around. They landed in some sort of museum, where every exhibit featured Bjorn T. Borgenson. Glass cases held the esteemed doctor's many awards. Pop-up holograms replayed moments from his life: Bjorn treating a patient, Bjorn reading to a roomful of children, Bjorn accepting yet another award . . .

22 ignored the question. "Look, I'm sure your life

was *ah-mazing* and you did *ah-mazing* things," she said sarcastically. "But here's what we're gonna do. We're going to stand here in silence for a little bit. Then we go back out, you say you tried, and I go back to not living my non-life. And *you* go to The Great Beyond."

Joe held up his hands. "No, look—"

"It's not going to work, anyway," 22 interrupted. "I've had thousands of mentors. I already know everything about Earth. And I don't want anything to do with it."

"Come on, now," Joe pleaded, trying to keep the desperation out of his voice. "Don't you want to fill out your pass? Earth has so much to offer."

"Eh." 22 shrugged. "I'm comfortable here. I have my routine. I float in mist. I do my Sudoku puzzles. And then, like, once a week they make me come to one of these seminars. It's not great, but I know what to expect."

Joe decided to level with her. "Look, kid . . . can I just be honest with you? I'm not Bjorn Borgenson. I'm not even a mentor!"

"Ah, reverse psychology! Ha!" 22 sneered. "You really are a good shrink, doctor."

"Argh!" Joe groaned in frustration. "Is there any way to show a different life in this place?"

22 eyed him suspiciously. She pulled a console up from the floor. Taking Joe's hand, she placed it flat on a scanner.

Instantly, the holograms of Bjorn Borgenson's life vanished. In their place sprang up scenes that looked curiously familiar to Joe.

"What the heck is all this?" 22 exclaimed.

"It's . . . my life," Joe said, gazing around in amazement.

22 peered into a glass case, where a bottle of cologne and a tube of breath spray were enshrined like historic artifacts. The placard read 1984: THE YEAR I DISCOVERED GIRLS.

Joe paused at a photo. In the picture, a teenage Joe stood awkwardly at a keyboard with three teen rappers posed next to him. "Cedric's rap group?" Joe said, cringing. "Man, who curated this exhibit?"

22 chuckled. "Heh. *You* did."

"Well, don't look at *that* stuff," Joe said, dragging her away. "Look over here!"

He pulled 22 over to a hologram, which was playing a memory like a short film. They watched Joe's father,

Ray Gardner, drag a twelve-year-old Joe into a jazz club.

"I don't wanna go!" young Joe protested. "I don't like jazz!"

"Black improvisational music is one of our great contributions to American culture," Ray lectured his son. "At least give it a chance, Joey!"

Inside the club, a jazz group was jamming. Young Joe stared at the pianist, watching his hands run up and down the keyboard and feeling the music swirl inside him. Watching it now, Joe felt the same thrill all over again.

"This is where it all started," Joe told 22. "This is the moment I fell in love with jazz. And because of that love, I became a jazz musician."

22 didn't reply. She was watching another hologram. In this one, Joe was getting fired from a gig at a jazz club.

"Wait—that's not how I remember that going down," Joe said. "I quit. I didn't get fired."

But in the next hologram, another club owner was showing Joe the door. And the next one. And the one after that.

Over and over again, Joe relived his life's failures. He watched himself conducting the middle-school

35

band. For the first time, Joe saw himself as nothing but a washed-up middle-aged musician.

They came to the last exhibit: Joe lying in a hospital bed. Next to him, a heart monitor slowly beeped.

"You're still alive?" 22 asked in surprise.

Joe gazed at his unconscious body. "My life was . . . worthless," he murmured. He straightened up and shook his head. "No," he decided. "*No!* I won't accept this." He turned to 22, eyeing her Personality Profile. "Kid, give me that badge."

"You want my badge?"

"You obviously don't want it," Joe said. "So just give it to me. Then I'll be out of your hair, and you can go annoy somebody else."

"Sure. Here." Just like that, 22 removed her Personality Profile and handed it to Joe.

But the moment he touched it, it vanished and reappeared on 22's chest. "Unless it becomes a full Earth Pass, I'm stuck with it," 22 explained.

"What if I help you turn it into an Earth Pass?" Joe suggested. "Would you give it to me then?"

22 considered. "I'd get to skip life—so, yes! But we've got to get this thing to change first. I've never been able to make it change."

It didn't sound that hard to Joe. "We've just got to find your Spark."

Joe brought up a hologram of his audition for Dorothea. "Today started out as the best day of my life. Because of *this*." They watched it right up to the moment Dorothea asked him to play. Joe felt pride and elation all over again.

22 was watching the scene with a glazed look. Joe glanced down at her Personality Profile. The last space was still blank. "Really? Nothing at all?"

22 shrugged. "It's not jazz. It's just . . . music. I don't like music sounds. It feels like a little much."

"Well, I'm not going out like this," Joe said with a sigh. "We've got to try something else. Where's that Hall of Everything?"

Seven

As 22 led Joe through the Soul World, they passed the Earth Portal.

"I'll be right back!" he called down to his home planet. "Don't go anywhere!"

"Don't get ahead of yourself, pal," 22 said.

Joe gritted his teeth. It was just his luck to get stuck with the most annoying soul to ever exist.

Before long, Joe and 22 had come to a massive corridor. Lined in rows on either side were every earthly thing imaginable. There were gardens, bulldozers, boats, cats, swimming pools, concert halls, elephants, cars, fishing poles, weaving looms, books, football fields, paintings, aquariums, guitars, telescopes, tree houses. . . . On and on and on it went. It was like being in a giant shopping mall—if a shopping mall contained every single thing in the world.

"Here we are. The Hall of Everything," 22 said.

All around them, new souls were exploring different activities. One new soul stood by a stream, casting a fishing rod while a mentor looked on. In another part of the hall, a new soul dribbled a basketball toward a net. A third new soul was fiddling with a camera. As the camera shutter clicked, the new soul's Personality Profile suddenly transformed into an Earth Pass.

Suddenly, Joe understood. These souls were figuring out what made life worth living. They were finding their Sparks, just like the counselors had said.

"Come on!" Joe grabbed 22's hand. Somewhere in here was a Spark for 22. He spied a bakery and pulled 22 toward it. Who didn't go crazy for butter and sugar?

Inside, aisles were lined with every baked good imaginable—cakes, cookies, tarts, pies, eclairs, croissants, and even pizza. He grabbed a steaming slice and held it out to 22. "Baking could be your Spark!"

"Yeah!" said 22. "But I don't get it."

"Just smell it!" Joe waved the pizza under her nose.

"I can't," 22 replied. "And neither can you."

Joe sniffed. 22 was right. He couldn't smell a thing.

Joe took a careful bite. Nothing. He gobbled down the whole slice, but there was no flavor, no heat, no texture. Even more disturbingly, the pizza slice came out his other end, fully formed.

"We can't taste, either?" Joe asked in dismay.

"All that stuff is in your body," 22 explained.

"No smell, no taste," Joe repeated. Somehow this made him feel even worse about being almost dead.

"Or touch." 22 reached out and slapped his face. Her hand met his cheek with a loud *smack*. Joe didn't feel a thing.

She slapped him again. And again. For the first time since Joe had met her, she seemed to be enjoying herself. A little too much, in fact.

"Okay! I get it," Joe snapped, dodging her hand. "Moving on."

They got to a burning building. Joe and 22 donned firefighter uniforms and helped douse the blaze. In an art studio, 22 tried oil painting. In a library, she tested out being a librarian. Scientist, dentist, glass blower, Olympic gymnast, astronaut—22 tried them all. She even tried being president of the United States! But nothing seemed to move her.

"Well," Joe said, when they'd worked their way through the entire hall, "I think that's everything." He was frustrated.

"Sorry," 22 said in a bored voice.

Joe glared at her. "You told me you'd try."

"What can I say, Joe?" she replied with a shrug. "Earth is boring."

"What else can we do, then?" Joe cried in exasperation. "We're running out of time!"

"Time's really not a thing here," 22 told him.

"Time's up!" exclaimed a voice nearby.

Joe jumped, startled. A counselor had suddenly appeared next to them.

"Nice try, Bjorn," the counselor said to Joe. "But no need to feel bad. 22 here can be a bit of a challenge." He patted 22 on the head.

She slapped his hand away. "Even though I can't feel it, please don't touch me."

The counselor turned to Joe. "Let's get you to The Great Beyond." Once again, the counselor opened a portal to the bright glowing light.

So *this is it,* Joe thought. *The last stop.* He couldn't believe he'd worked his whole life just to have it end this way.

"Wait!" 22 cried. To Joe's astonishment, she leaped between him and the counselor. "We forgot to try, uh . . . birthday clown! I think that's going to be my thing. Kinda fun, kinda terrifying? Can we have one more minute to try birthday clown? Please, Jerry? You look really good today, Jerry!"

The counselor looked surprised. "I've never seen 22 this enthused. Good for you, Dr. Borgenson," he said with a smile. He vanished as suddenly as he'd appeared.

As soon as he was gone, 22 turned to Joe. "Run!" she said.

She sprinted off, and Joe raced after her.

They came to a beat-up cardboard box lying on the ground. A sign posted next to it read JUST A BOX.

"In here!" 22 ducked down and crawled inside the box. Joe followed and emerged into 22's clubhouse. It was full of old junk that 22 had collected. One wall was covered in hundreds of name tags from her past mentors.

22 led Joe to a portal located under a kitchen sink. "Here it is!"

"Where does it lead?" Joe asked warily.

"Hey, you ask too many questions," 22 retorted. "How about you zip it for a minute?"

"And we're going there why?" Joe asked, ignoring her suggestion.

"Because I know a guy," 22 told him. "A guy who can help. A guy like *you.*"

Joe's eyes widened. "Like me. As in . . . *alive?*"

22 nodded.

"Are you actually helping me?" Joe asked, confused.

"Joe, I have been living here for who knows how long, and I've never seen anything that makes me want to live," 22 told him. "And then you come along. Your life is so sad and pathetic. And you're working so hard to get it back. Why?" Her face brightened. "This I gotta see!"

Her attitude wasn't exactly pleasant, but it gave Joe a glimmer of hope. "Let's go!"

Eight

Joe was starting to think nothing could surprise him in the Soul World. But once again, he could hardly believe his eyes.

Before them stretched a vast, rolling landscape. The sky was filled with swirls of pink, purple, and blue. Waves of glittering black sand rose and fell beneath their feet. Joe felt like he was stepping into the sand dunes of a psychedelic dream.

"What *is* this place?" Joe murmured, awestruck.

"I used to call it Loserville," 22 said with a bored shrug. "But my buddy says it's the Astral Plane. You know when you humans are really into something and it feels like you're in another place? You're in the Zone, right?"

"Uh, yeah?" said Joe, still not sure what she was getting at.

"Well, *this* is the Zone," 22 said, leading him forward. "It's the place between the physical and the spiritual."

"I was here!" Joe exclaimed. "Today at my audition! This must be where musicians come when they get in a flow."

"Not just musicians," 22 said. Looking around, Joe saw she was right. He saw a chef, an actor, a dancer, and even an accountant. They were all immersed in their craft and lost to the world.

As they crossed over a hill, they saw a herd of creatures moving toward them. The strange beasts lumbered along on twisted legs. Their bodies were coated in layers of black grime. From out of the filth, a single roving eye peered like a headlight.

Suddenly, one of the headlights swiveled toward Joe and 22. The creature looked at them for a second. Then it charged.

"Run!" cried 22.

They tried to flee, but it was like running in a nightmare—they couldn't get away. The sand shifted beneath their feet, slowing them down. The creature was nearly upon them—

SNAP! A hidden trap shot up from the ground and closed around the beast. A small bell on top of it rang.

DING! DING! Across the astral sands, a massive wooden ship came sailing toward them, its bell chiming. It looked like a pirate ship with wildly tie-dyed sails. Atop the crow's nest, a peace-sign pennant snapped in the wind.

As the ship got closer, an anchor sailed over the side and landed in the sand next to Joe and 22. The ship jerked to a halt. A face peeked over the side. Like Joe's, his was luminescent, but with a handlebar mustache and long, bushy hair.

"Ahoy there, fellow astral travelers!" the soul called down to them. "Good to see you again, 22!"

"Moonwind! How's the wife and kids?" she called back.

"Churlish and combative!" he replied cheerfully.

"Hey, I got a request for you," 22 said to the soul. She nudged Joe.

"Uh . . . yeah," Joe said. "I'm trying to get back to my body. Can you help me?"

"That's what we do!" Moonwind replied.

A gangplank appeared over the side of the ship.

Moonwind started down it, followed by the souls of two women and one man.

"We are the Mystics Without Borders," Moonwind explained. "Devoted to helping the lost souls of Earth find their way. I'm Moonwind Stardancer, at your service." Moonwind gave a little bow. Then he pointed to the other souls. "That's Windstar Dreamermoon, Dancerstar Windmoon, and that's Dreamerwind Dreamerdreamer."

They nodded and waved at Joe.

"These weirdos are going to help me get back to Earth?" Joe asked 22. He suddenly felt a lot less confident.

The soul called Dancerstar went over to the trapped creature. "Let's get this lost soul back home," she said.

She freed it from the net. Then the mystics brought out long brushes and buckets of soapy water and began scrubbing the lost soul.

As the gritty black stuff was washed away, a soul emerged. He looked around at them all, blinking in confusion. "Where am I?"

"Poor fellow," said Moonwind. "Some people just can't let go of their own anxieties and obsessions, leaving them lost and disconnected from life. And this is the result." He squinted at the soul. "Looks like another hedge-fund manager."

"Now to reconnect to your earthly form," Dancerstar said. She drew a circle in the sand with her walking stick. A hole opened. To Joe's amazement, he could see down to Earth. And not just the planet. He could see right into an office building on Wall Street, where a fortyish man was hunched over his desk. Around him, computer screens dripped numbers.

"Whoa! That's me! Thank you!" The hedge-fund manager's soul leaped into the portal.

Down on Earth, the hedge-fund manager woke from his trance. "What am I doing with my life?" he asked aloud.

The man leaped to his feet. He pushed the computers and monitors off his own desk, and then off the desks of his astonished colleagues. "I'm alive! I'm alive! Free yourselves. Ha-ha!" he cried, dancing out the door.

"He got back? Just like that?" Joe grabbed Moonwind's walking stick and drew another circle in the sand. "So this is all I have to do to get back to my body?"

As the hole opened for him, Joe prepared to jump.

But it wasn't Earth that appeared. Instead, he saw the humming white light of The Great Beyond.

Joe and the mystics moved back from the edge. "Egad, man!" Moonwind cried, quickly throwing sand over it. He looked at Joe carefully. "Joe, are you . . . dead?"

"No!" Joe said. "Not yet. I'm just in a coma. But you can help me get back."

"We've never connected an untethered soul back to its body before," said Moonwind.

"Is that even possible?" Dancerstar asked.

Moonwind stroke his beard thoughtfully. "Perhaps if we travel to a thin spot . . ." His face lit up with excitement. "All aboard!"

Ding! Ding! The ship sailed across the Astral Plane and over more herds of lost souls. Joe wondered aloud how they got that way.

"They become Lost Souls when they become obsessed with any one thing," Moonwind explained. "Even I used to be a Lost Soul—I used to play too much *Tetris.*"

Joe looked around at his fellow passengers. "So, if your souls are here, where are your bodies?" he asked.

"On Earth, of course!" Moonwind said.

"My body is in a trance in Palawan," Windstar explained.

"I'm playing the Saraswati veena in Quebec," Dancerstar volunteered.

"I'm a shamanic healer in Marin, California," Dreamerwind added.

"Let me guess," Joe said to Moonwind. "You're drumming, chanting, and meditating?"

"Yes . . . something like that," Moonwind replied. "I'm in New York City, on the corner of 14th and 7th."

"Oh, that's just up from the Good Stuff Diner!" Joe said. This guy wasn't just any weirdo; he was a New York City weirdo. Somehow, Joe found this comforting.

"Yes, precisely. We mystics meet in this glorious landscape every Tuesday," Moonwind explained.

"The fact is, everyone comes here," Dancerstar said. "Most don't even know it."

"Ah, if only these people could open their eyes, oh the places they'd go!" said Moonwind.

The ship slowed and Moonwind threw down the anchor, scattering a group of lost souls. Then he led Joe, 22, and the rest of the crew down the gangplank.

Joe sat as Moonwind drew a circle in the sand.

The mystics formed another circle around him. Dreamerwind passed out instruments—drums, a rainstick, castanets. She handed a tambourine to 22, who looked at it like it was radioactive.

"Now, since you don't have a connection to your body, you will have to tune back into your physical surroundings," Moonwind instructed. He began to beat on a bongo drum. "Close your eyes. Breathe into your crown chakra."

Joe wasn't sure what a crown chakra was, but he was willing to try anything. He closed his eyes. He breathed deeply. He imagined his soul returning to his body. It wasn't easy. The racket coming from the mystics rivaled that of the M.S. 74 school band.

"Do we really need all this?" he asked, opening his eyes.

"Yes!" exclaimed Moonwind.

Joe closed his eyes and tried again. But he couldn't locate any chakras, crown or otherwise.

He opened his eyes. "Do you have a piano on board? I could focus with that!"

"No pianos, Joe!" Moonwind exclaimed. "You must focus! Concentrate on where your body is."

Joe did as he said. He breathed slowly in and out.

He imagined his soul leaving the Astral Plane and soaring down toward Earth. He could see the scrim of clouds above it.

Now he was hovering above New York City, looking down on it as if from an airplane.

"Concentrate on where your body is," Moonwind said. "Listen for cues."

Now he could hear the sounds of traffic. He could see the grid of the streets.

"That's it! You're doing it!" cried Moonwind, playing faster.

Joe opened his eyes. At once, the view fell away, as if he were speeding backward.

"No peeking," Moonwind told Joe. "Maintain your meditative state or you'll break the connection."

Joe obeyed, closing his eyes once again, and the view of New York swooped in, closer than ever. He seemed to be hovering over the hospital where his body lay.

"See if you can smell and feel where your body is," Moonwind intoned.

Joe concentrated. "I hear . . . an air conditioner." He breathed in a sharp odor. "I can smell . . . hand sanitizer."

Slowly but surely, his senses were awakening. "I

think I can feel my feet!" And there was something soft under his hand, something that didn't seem to belong in a hospital. "I feel . . . fur?"

On Earth, Joe's body moved its lips. "I . . . feel . . . fur," he murmured. His hand, which was resting on a therapy cat, twitched.

In the Astral Plane, Joe couldn't wait any longer. "When can I jump in? Am I close?" Joe opened his eyes. "Hey! Look! There I am!"

But at that moment, the view began to drop away. Earth was receding from him once again.

"No! No!" Joe cried. "What are we waiting for?" He stood up and moved toward the hole.

"Joe! Don't rush this! It's not the right time!" Moonwind cried, trying to hold him back.

"It's my time!" Shaking his arm free of Moonwind's grip, Joe charged for the hole. In his rush, he knocked against 22.

The last thing Joe heard was 22 cry, "Wait! Not me!" as they plummeted toward the hospital room.

Nine

Joe opened his eyes. The Astral Plane was gone, and so were Moonwind and the other mystics. He was alone in a room. He saw walls painted a muted yellow. He smelled a sharp antiseptic scent. He could hear the hum of an air conditioner and the beeping of a heart monitor.

"I did it! I'm back!" he exclaimed.

Joe struggled to sit up, wondering why his body wasn't cooperating. Then Joe's gaze fell on his hands. They didn't look like his own hands. They didn't look like hands at all. They were paws.

Joe looked down at his body. It was covered in calico fur.

"No!" Joe gasped. "I'm in the cat?"

He turned to look at the body lying beside him. It was *his* body—he saw his own head resting against a pillow, his face slack. His eyelids were twitching, as if he was starting to wake up.

"Wait a minute," Joe said, "if *I'm* in the cat, then who . . ."

Joe felt utterly surreal as he watched his own body open his eyes. "Uhh . . . what . . . ," he heard 22's voice say.

"*You're* in my body?" Joe cried, aghast. *No, no, no! How could this all have gone so wrong?*

22 stared back at him through Joe's face. She looked as horrified as Joe felt.

"You're in the *cat*?"

"Why are you in my body?" Joe demanded.

22 lifted her arms and gaped at the hands hanging from her wrists. Human hands. "I'm in a body! Blech, it's disgusting!" she cried.

"I don't want to be in a cat. I hate cats! That Moonwind guy—he messed this up!" Joe exclaimed.

At that moment, a doctor and a nurse entered the room, followed by an older woman holding a cat carrier.

"Doc, you've got to help me!" Joe pleaded. "That's my body, but I'm trapped in this cat!"

The doctor, the nurse, and the cat lady stared back at him, not comprehending.

"Oh, no!" Joe gasped, realizing. "They can't understand me. They think you're me! You gotta try."

As the doctor lifted Joe's arm to take his pulse, 22 cleared her throat. "Uh, Ms. Doctor?" she said through Joe's mouth. "We have a problem. I'm an unborn soul and I want to stay at the You Seminar."

The doctor frowned. She made a note on her clipboard.

"*Shhhh!*" Joe told 22. "They're going to think you're nuts! I mean . . . that *I'm* nuts. Ugh. How did this happen?"

"I fell into your body because it doesn't have a soul," 22 hissed at him.

"Then why am I in a cat?" Joe asked.

"I don't know!" she exclaimed.

The doctor watched this conversation with obvious concern. "Is there anyone we can call, Mr. Gardner? A next of kin or a friend?" she asked.

"Tell her no!" Joe commanded.

"Uh . . . no!" 22 made Joe's body say.

"Can you tell me what day it is?" the doctor asked.

"It's the worst day of my life!" 22 replied. "I don't want to be here! I hate Earth!"

"Tell you what," the doctor said slowly. "We're going to keep you here for observation. Just for a bit." She reached for the cat. "Perhaps our therapy cat can go to his next appointment—"

HISS! Joe swiped a claw at the doctor. He wasn't going anywhere until he was back in his own body!

"Okay! Okay!" The doctor backed off.

"You've got to talk to her!" Joe told 22.

22 took a deep breath. "Uh, Ms. Doctor? This body's soul is in this cat—"

"Stop talking," Joe ordered.

"So naturally he wants to stay close," 22 finished.

"Keep the cat," the doctor said. "Just get some rest. A lot of it, okay?"

The doctor and nurse headed for the door. The cat lady picked up the cat carrier. "I'll come get Mr. Mittens in ten minutes," she said before following them out.

"Ten minutes!" Joe cried when they were gone. "We've got to get out of here!"

"No way. I am not moving!" 22 replied. She looked down at Joe's body in disgust. "I can't believe I'm in a body! On this hellish planet! I have bendy meat sticks!" She flexed Joe's fingers in revulsion. "I can feel myself feeling myself."

"Focus!" Joe cried, batting her with a paw. "Listen to me! We've got to get out of here before they take me away."

"Take you away?" 22 cried. "You're gonna leave me?"

"No way. That's my body you're in! Okay." Joe took a deep breath. "Do you think you can walk?"

"I don't know!" 22 wailed. "I failed Body Test Drive, like, four hundred and thirty-six times!"

Oh brother, Joe thought. "But will you try?"

22 paused, as if considering her options. Finally, she nodded.

"We've got to find Moonwind. He can fix this." Joe rose on his four legs. He looked down at the floor. It seemed like a long, *long* way down.

"I'm a cat," Joe assured himself. "I can make this."

Joe leaped, stretching his feet out before him. He belly-flopped onto the linoleum.

22 wasn't much better off. She had made it up from the bed and now stood teetering on Joe's legs as if they were stilts. Holding out her arms for balance, she took a tentative step. Then another . . .

22 made it as far as the chair next to the bed. She collapsed into it face-first.

"I'm just going to rest here for a minute," she mumbled.

"No! Come on!" Joe swatted her legs to get her moving. "They'll be back any minute!"

They lurched into the hallway, Joe scrambling on his slippery paws, 22 staggering on her unfamiliar legs. Thankfully, the corridor was empty. Joe spotted a green EXIT sign ahead. Just a few more feet and they would be out!

They had almost reached it when Joe saw the doctor coming toward them. But her face was down as she looked at something on her clipboard.

"In here!" Joe shoved 22 through an open doorway. She fell into a hospital bed, much to the surprise of the patient lying there.

As soon as the doctor was gone, Joe pushed 22 out of the bed. They staggered toward the elevator.

"Good," Joe said when they got there. "Now push the 'down' button."

22 tried. But she wasn't used to having fingers. Over and over she poked at the panel without once managing to actually hit the button.

"Careful! Those fingers are my livelihood!" Frustrated, Joe leaped into 22's arms and hit the elevator button with his paw.

Ding! The elevator doors opened. "Get in," Joe commanded.

22 stumbled into the elevator. As soon as the doors closed, she slid down to the floor with a sigh of relief.

"Okay. What did Moonwind say?" Joe asked, climbing down from her arms. "Corner of Fourteenth and Seventh?"

"That's Chelsea," 22 replied. "Near Jackson Square Park."

"How do you know that?" Joe asked, startled.

"It's all in this stupid brain of yours," 22 replied, tapping a finger on Joe's head.

"Hey! Stay out of there!" Joe exclaimed. The last thing he wanted was 22 poking around in his private thoughts.

22 rolled her eyes. "Oh, relax. There's not much here. Jazz, jazz, jazz, more jazz."

The elevator doors opened. Ahead, Joe could see a stretch of shining tile floor, and beyond that, the frosted glass doors that led to freedom.

Joe led the way across the lobby. They were almost there!

But as they reached the door, 22 paused. She stood there, swaying on Joe's legs.

"This is all happening too fast," she said. "Let's just take a minute and—"

"Come on, let's go!" Joe glanced nervously over his shoulder, expecting to see doctors and nurses rushing toward them. "They could be here any minute."

Joe jumped down to open the automatic doors, then leaped into 22's arms and steered her outside.

On the city street, the noise hit them like a wave. Cabs honked. Fire trucks wailed. Jackhammers pounded. Buildings rose dizzyingly overhead. Crowds of people rushed past on the sidewalk.

Joe felt 22's arms tense around him. She tried to back away, but she was swept into the crowd and carried along the sidewalk.

"Just keep walking," Joe told her.

They were halfway across the street when 22 suddenly froze, too frightened to take another step. People moved around them, jostling them in their annoyance.

Then the light turned green. Four lanes of cars started forward, coming right toward them!

"Don't stop!" Joe screeched. "This is New York. Don't just stop in the middle of the street. Go, go, *GO*!"

He pawed desperately at 22, trying to get her moving. But he'd forgotten that his paws had *claws*.

22 shrieked as his claws sank in. She dropped Joe and raced across the street, weaving through the traffic.

"Oh, no," Joe gasped. "22!" She'd disappeared into the crowd on the other side of the street.

Joe raced down the sidewalk, dodging the feet of pedestrians. He tried to spot 22 in the crowd, but all he saw was a sea of ankles. From his cat's-eye view, the busy sidewalk seemed like a jungle of moving trees.

Joe ran up and down the block. At last, he spotted a man in a hospital gown huddled in a doorway. The man's face was buried in his arms, but Joe recognized his own body at once. With a sigh of relief, he hurried over to it.

22 looked up as he approached. Joe saw that she was shaking.

"Look, I didn't know I had claws. I'm sorry," he told 22. "Now come on—let's go."

22 wouldn't budge. "No way. I'm staying here until your stupid body dies! Which will happen any minute now, because your stomach is earthquaking."

Joe gaped at her in confusion. Stomach? Earthquake? What was she talking about?

Suddenly, it clicked—22 was hungry!

That gave Joe an idea. Leaving 22 in the doorway, he hurried around the corner to a nearby pizza joint. Joe waited outside until two people entered. Then he slipped through the door behind them.

Ahhh! The aroma of pizza made his whiskers twitch with pleasure. Joe was glad to discover he could still enjoy it—even as a cat.

Joe slinked around the side of the counter. While the server was busy taking an order, he reached up a paw and swiped a pepperoni slice. He carried it back to 22 in his teeth.

She hadn't moved from her spot. She looked more miserable than ever.

"This place is worse than I thought," 22 complained. "It's loud and bright and—" She paused, sniffing the air. "What's that in my nose?"

"That's smell," Joe told her. He waved the slice, wafting the odor toward her enticingly.

22 looked at it with interest.

"If you think that's good, just imagine what it tastes like." He held the slice out. "Go on."

22 took a tentative bite. Her eyes widened in amazement. "It's . . . not horrible," she said. 22 began to gobble the pizza like a starving wolf. When she was done, she licked her fingers. "Strange—I don't feel so angry anymore."

"Great. Ready to find Moonwind now?" Joe asked.

"That depends," 22 said, standing. "Do you have any more hot triangles?"

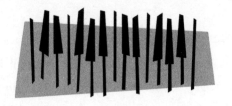

Ten

Very quickly, Joe discovered that the way to 22's feet was through her stomach. As long as he kept her stomach full, her feet kept moving.

Two more slices of pizza and one gyro later, they had almost made it to Chelsea. Joe rode on 22's shoulders, steering her impatiently as she munched on the dripping sandwich.

"I'm telling you, Joe," 22 gabbed between bites, "It's pronounced *yee*-row."

"It's New York. We call them *gy*-ros. It's Greek," Joe said distractedly. They had reached the corner of 14th Street and 7th Avenue. But where was Moonwind?

22 licked the last of the sauce off her fingers. "Huh," she said. "That's not how Archimedes pronounced it."

On the far corner, a balding man with a mustache and goatee was spinning a sign in front of a discount cell phone store. With his eyes closed, he moved to the music on his headphones, flipping the cardboard sign with the grace of a baton twirler. He looked like he was in the Zone.

"That's gotta be him," Joe said, urging 22 across the street.

"Moonwind!" 22 ran up to the man and grabbed his arm. "Moonwind! You gotta help me!"

Moonwind opened his eyes, looking dazed. But when he saw 22, his face lit up.

"Joe!" he exclaimed. "You made it into your body!"

"No, he didn't," 22 replied.

"*That* is my body," Joe said, pointing his paw at 22.

"You're in a cat?" Moonwind looked delighted. "That's marvelous!"

Wait, Joe thought in surprise, *Moonwind can understand me?* Then again, if any human on the planet could understand a cat, it was bound to be Moonwind.

"Hey, Moonwimp!" an angry voice interrupted. A middle-aged woman with purple hair stormed out of the cell phone store. "That sign won't spin itself, hear me?"

"But, Marge, look!" Moonwind cried. "I put this man's soul in a cat!"

The scowl on Marge's face deepened. "Who cares? And you"—she turned to glare at Joe and 22—"we only have room for one weirdo here, so scram!"

Marge spun on her spiky heels and stomped back into the store.

"No one understands my art," Moonwind grumbled. With a sigh, he picked up his sign and began to spin it again.

"Moonwind, listen!" Joe said. "I've got to get out of *here*," he gestured to his cat body. "And back in *there*."

"Oh! Well, we'll have to perform an old-fashioned astral transmigration displacement," Moonwind replied.

"A what?" asked Joe.

"It's simply a way to get your souls back where they belong," Moonwind explained. "And it's a glorious ritual indeed, full of chanting, dancing, and—best of all—bongos!"

Not the bongos again, Joe thought. "I need to be at The Half Note by seven, so this needs to happen right now," he told Moonwind.

"Whoa, whoa, not so fast! You must wait for

another thin spot to open between Earth and the Astral Plane," Moonwind said. "And that won't occur until Orcus moves into the house of the Gemini."

"When is that?" Joe asked, exasperated.

"Well, the government calls it *six-thirty*," Moonwind said with a roll of his eyes. "I'll meet you at The Half Note. I'll even gather all of the necessary provisions—"

He broke off as Marge stormed out of the store again, hands on her hips. "I said get out of here! Go!" she yelled at 22.

22 took off running, with Joe still on her shoulders.

"And stay away!" Marge hollered.

"See you at The Half Note at six-thirty!" Moonwind called after them. "I'll take care of everything!"

"Six-thirty is cutting it close. Too close," Joe said as they headed down street.

22 nodded, only half listening. She was busy downing her fourth slice of pizza.

"That's the last snack," Joe told her sternly. "I can barely fit into my pants as it is. We've got to get back to my place and get you—I mean, *me*—cleaned up and ready to go. We need to hail a cab."

Joe scanned the street. He spied several yellow cabs in the sea of traffic. "Hold out your hand," he told 22.

She did as he asked. But cab after cab passed them by. No one wanted to pick up a man in a hospital gown wearing a cat like a fur stole.

Joe prayed for a miracle. And just when he was about to despair, his prayer was answered. A cab pulled up to the curb a few feet away to let out passengers.

"Go!" Joe shouted at 22. "Go, go, go! Just run to that one!" If they could slip into the backseat before the driver saw them, they'd be set.

22 stumbled over to the cab just as the door opened. And Dorothea Williams stepped out.

"Is that . . . Teach?" For one long, horrible moment, Dorothea gaped at her new piano player. Her eyes traveled from his face to his bare legs and hospital gown, then back up to the cat wrapped around his shoulders.

Joe didn't know what to do except hide. He dove into the backseat of the taxicab, pulling 22 in after him. The door slammed shut.

As the cab pulled away, Joe peeked out the back window. Dorothea was still standing there, staring after them.

Eleven

"Ugh!" Joe cried for the hundredth time. "Dorothea Williams saw me! What am I going to do? She's going to think I'm crazy!"

They climbed the steps to Joe's apartment building. 22 was busy with another piece of pizza.

"Maybe you should call her up and tell her that we're not crazy!" Joe suggested.

"I've only been a person for an hour, and even I know that's a bad idea," 22 replied.

22 opened the door to Joe's apartment, then quickly shut it behind her, collapsing against it with a sigh of relief.

Joe leaped down from her shoulders and paced the floor, trying to think if there was any possible way to save the situation. "I've just got to get back in my body and really bring it tonight," he decided.

22 didn't reply. When Joe looked over, he saw she had her nose in her armpit, busily sniffing.

"How come this part is stinky? But this part smells fine?" she asked, pointing to Joe's forearm.

"Never mind." Joe flicked his tail toward a pile of dirty laundry. "Just put those pants on. I can't believe I've been walking around in this city with no pants on."

"I don't even want to be here, remember!" 22 said as she struggled to pull up the pants. At last she managed to get them on. Backward.

Joe paced through a patch of sunlight. "I don't want you here, either. . . ." A huge yawn overtook him. The sunlight was having a strange effect on him. His entire body seemed to melt into a small furry puddle. He couldn't keep his eyes open.

"I just want to . . . get my body back . . . and get back to the . . . club," Joe murmured between yawns. He flopped down in the warm square of light, purring.

Bzzzz! Bzzzzz! The sound of his cell phone jerked Joe out of his doze.

"Your clothes are rumbling again," 22 said. She pulled the buzzing phone from the pocket of the hospital gown.

Joe lunged and tried to grab it, forgetting once again that he had paws. The phone flipped like a cat toy as he batted it with his furry mitts. It clattered to the ground and fell silent.

Joe saw four missed calls from Curley. He groaned. Whatever Curley had to say, it couldn't be good. With a sinking feeling, Joe played the voice mail.

"Hey, Mr. G. It's Curley. Um . . . I hope you're doing okay. Dorothea freaked out when she saw you. And she called this other guy, Robert. He's got the gig now. Sorry."

"No, no, no!" Joe wailed.

There was a pause, then Curley continued. *"Honestly, your class was the only reason I went to school at all. I owe you a lot. So, here's the plan. Clean yourself up, put on a killer suit, and get to the club early. I'm going to try to talk to her."*

Joe gasped. He still had a chance!

"Just make sure you show up looking like a million bucks, all right? I hope to see you, man. Peace."

"I can get the gig back!" Joe cried. "22, I need your help! I have a suit. I'm going to need you to try it on. And then I can line up my hair a little bit, and—"

"No," 22 cut him off. "Nope. No way!"

"22!" Joe glared at her.

22 glared right back.

A loud pounding made them both jump. Someone was knocking on the door. "Mr. Gardner?" said a young girl's voice.

"It's Connie." Joe waved a paw dismissively. "She's here for her lesson."

22 eyed the door nervously. "What do I do?"

"Just ignore her," Joe told her. "Connie's not part of the plan."

22 went over to the door. "Hi, Connie. Sorry, but Joe can't do it today," she called. "I mean me . . . me can't do it today."

Connie probably thought he'd lost his marbles, but Joe was beyond caring. The only thing that mattered now was getting his body to The Half Note on time.

"Now let's go check out that suit—" he began.

"I came to tell you that I quit!" Connie called through the door.

"Quit?" 22 looked intrigued.

"In fact," Connie added, "all of band is a stupid waste of time!"

"This kid is talking sense!" 22 started to open the dead bolt.

"What are you doing?" Joe cried.

73

But it was too late. 22 cracked the door open and peered out over the chain. Connie was standing in the hallway. Her arms were crossed, and her face looked sullen. A black trombone case sat at her feet.

When she saw her band teacher, Connie picked up the trombone and held it out. "Here. I quit. I think jazz is pointless."

"Oh, yeah," 22 agreed, nodding vigorously. "Jazz is definitely pointless."

"Hey!" Joe protested.

Connie didn't even look his way. All she'd heard was a cat yowling. "In fact," she went on, "all of school is a waste of time."

"Of course!" 22 agreed. "Like my mentor George Orwell used to say, state-sponsored education is like the rattling of a stick inside a swill bucket."

Connie's eyes widened in surprise. "Yeah!"

"The ruling class's core curriculum stifles dissent," 22 went on. "It's the oldest trick in the book."

"What are you talking about?" Joe snapped. "She doesn't care about any of that!"

"I've been saying that since the third grade!" Connie cried in delight.

22 narrowed her eyes at the preteen. "You know,

you seem really smart. But tell me this: What is your position on pizza?"

"Um . . . I like it?" said Connie.

"Me too!" 22 unchained the door and flung it open. "I'd rather hang with Connie," she told Joe.

22 stepped into the hallway, shutting the door in Joe's face.

"Hey! Come back here! You open this door! Don't you walk away from me!" Joe cried.

Out in the hallway, Connie looked at the door. She could hear Joe's muffled yowls. "Uh, I think your cat wants to get out," she told 22.

"Ugh." 22 rolled her eyes. "He thinks he knows everything."

Inside, Joe scratched at the doorframe. He leaped over and over for the doorknob, but it was no use. He couldn't open it with his paws.

Joe peeked through the crack underneath the door. He could see Connie and 22 sitting on the stairs.

"I'd better give this back," Connie said, handing over the trombone case. "It belongs to the school."

22 took the case and set it aside. But Connie looked as though she'd just given away her dog.

"You know, I'm really glad there's someone else who

sees how ridiculous this place is," 22 told Connie. "I mean, anyone can make trumpet sounds—"

"You know what, Mr. G?" Connie interrupted suddenly. She opened the case and took out the trombone. "I was practicing this thing yesterday, and . . . well, maybe you can listen to it and tell me to quit after, okay?"

"Uh, okay," replied 22.

Connie played a heartfelt solo on her trombone. When she was finished, she looked at her teacher for his reaction.

"Wow," 22 said quietly. "You really love this."

"Yeah," Connie admitted. "So maybe I'd better stick with it?"

22 nodded. "Yeah."

Joe had gone back to jumping for the knob when suddenly the door opened, knocking him to the floor. 22 came back in. He heard Connie call, "Bye, Mr. G!" as she headed down the stairs.

Finally! Joe thought. Now they could get on with getting his body cleaned up.

But 22 seemed lost in thought. "So, Connie came here to quit, but then she didn't. I need to know this, Joe: Why didn't she quit?"

"Because she loves to play," Joe explained impatiently. "She might say she hates everything, but trombone is her thing and she's good at it. Maybe trombone is her Spark, I don't know. *Please, 22*." If Joe had had hands, he would have clasped them together. "If I'm going to get this gig back, I need your help."

22 looked at him for a moment. She took a deep breath. "Okay."

"Really?" Joe said, startled. He'd expected more of a fight.

"I'll help you. But I . . ." 22 paused, as if she was searching for the right words. "I want to try a few things. It's not like the Hall of Everything here. It's realer. If Connie can find something she loves here, maybe I can, too."

"Great!" Joe exclaimed.

"So . . . what do we do first?" 22 asked.

It took almost an hour, and a lot of coaching from Joe, but at last they managed to get 22 showered and dressed in Joe's only suit. As Joe sat on 22's shoulders, checking out their reflection in the mirror, he thought he didn't look half bad.

"Trusty old brown suit," Joe said. He leaned over,

attempting to tie the tie with his paws. "Still a perfect fit."

"It's a little tight in the back-here part." 22 pointed at the seat of his pants.

"It'll loosen," Joe told her. "Now sit down."

22 took a seat on the floor. Joe put a towel around her neck. Then, standing on his hind legs, he pushed a stack of records over to her to use as a stool.

When he had everything arranged, Joe picked up his hair clippers and turned them on.

22 held her hand out. "I'll do it."

"You couldn't call an elevator, remember? No way. This is my hair. I just need to line me up. Be still."

Joe climbed atop the pile of records. He leaned toward 22's head, intending to shave just around the edges of his hair. But he was having trouble holding the clippers in his paws.

22's eyes widened in alarm. "It looks like a tiny chain saw!"

"Don't move!" Joe commanded.

"I'm not moving. *You're* moving!" she exclaimed.

Sure enough, Joe's entire furry body was vibrating along with the clippers.

He managed to steady himself and tightened his

grip. 22 closed her eyes, like she was afraid to look.

Just as the clippers touched his hair, the record Joe was standing on slipped out from under him. He scrambled for footing, but the whole tower of records had started to collapse. The clippers flew from his paws, carved a trench through 22's hair, then hit the floor and shattered.

"Ahhhh!" Joe screamed.

"Don't worry," 22 said. "I'm okay."

"No, my *hair*!" Joe yelled. "My hair is not okay! This is a disaster!"

22 examined her reflection in the mirror. "Yeesh," she agreed.

"We've got to fix this!" Joe cried. "We've got to go see Dez."

"Okay!" 22 said helpfully. Then she frowned. "Who's Dez?"

Dez was the best barber in New York City. He was always booked solid, so Joe knew that they would have to get in on a wing and a prayer.

But Joe didn't have time to explain all that. He just threw a hat at 22 and headed for the door.

Twelve

Back at the You Seminar, business carried on as usual. The Jerrys herded new souls this way and that, sending them through the Personality Pavilions. At that moment, Terry the accountant came scurrying toward them. She was holding a thin folder above her head, waving it like a prize.

"Found him!" Terry crowed. "See that, everybody? Who figured out why the count's off? That's right, Terry did! It's Terrytime!" She did a little victory dance.

The Jerrys waited patiently for her to finish. "Well, who is it?" one finally asked.

"Right. Ahem." Terry ceremoniously opened the file. "Joe Gardner is his name. It looks like he's back down on Earth."

"That's not good," said the first Jerry, looking at the photo.

"That's the mentor we set up with 22," the other Jerry agreed.

"All right, all right. Easy on the hysterics," Terry said. "Terry's got this under control. I'll handle it."

"How?" asked the counselors.

"I'll go down there and get him. Set the count right, lickety-split." Terry dusted her hands to show how easy it would be.

"Are you sure that's a good idea?" the counselor asked. The counselors never went to Earth. Earth was for humans. The counselors' only job was to prepare souls for life. After that, they didn't get involved. Certainly the accountant couldn't go, either.

"Look, you all are the ones who beefed it," Terry snapped. "I'm trying to *un*-beef it."

The Jerrys exchanged helpless looks. They both tried to think of a better idea. Neither one could.

At last, they gave nods of consent. "But you cannot be seen," the first Jerry said sternly.

"By anyone," the other Jerry added.

"Don't worry," Terry said. "I'll make sure no one else sees me. I'll move among the shadows, like a ninja."

She smiled to herself. "I'm going to enjoy bringing this one in."

"Please, just do it quickly and quietly." The counselors already looked like they were regretting their decision.

Terry gave a "Roger" salute. She opened a portal to Earth, then slipped through and vanished.

The Jerrys stood together in worried silence.

"Well," one said at last, "this won't be a disaster. That's for sure."

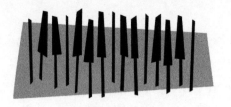

Thirteen

Joe and 22 stood on the sidewalk, peering through the window of Buddy's Barbershop. The shop was crowded with customers.

"Dez is the guy in the back," Joe said, pointing out a broad-shouldered man with tattooed arms and a thick beard. "Talk about having a Spark! This guy was born to be a barber."

22 nervously fingered the notch in her hair. "But I can't pass for you in front of all your friends!"

"Dez is the only one I talk to," Joe assured her. "We usually talk about jazz. But this time just sit there, get the cut, and get out."

He gestured for 22 to hurry up. 22 put her hat back on and walked into the shop with the cat still sitting on her shoulders.

As the bell on the door rang, everyone looked up. The other customers nodded silently to Joe, then went back to their conversations.

"Hey, Joe. What are you doing here on a weekday?" Dez said when he saw him. Another customer was just getting seated in his chair. "You didn't call for an appointment, man. It's gonna be a while."

Joe's heart sank. "Aw, I was afraid of this," he murmured to 22. "Sit down."

22 went over to a chair against the wall and sat down. Without thinking, she took off the hat.

There was a collective gasp from everyone in the barbershop.

"Oh my lawd!" Dez shooed the other customer out of his chair, exclaiming, "You've got to wait, son. This is an emergency! Joe, get your butt in this seat. Now."

22 hurried over and sat down. Still sitting on 22's shoulders, Joe breathed a sigh of relief. Miracle granted.

"Should I even ask how this happened?" Dez asked, eyeing the divot in 22's hair.

"The cat did it," she told him.

"Stop sounding insane!" Joe snapped.

"I mean, I was distracted getting ready to play with Dorothea Williams tonight," 22 said quickly.

Dez's face lit up. "Dorothea Williams? That's big-time, Joe! Congratulations!"

"Joe ain't getting no gig, Dez," sneered the customer in the next chair over. "You know he's Mr. Close-But-No-Cigar."

"Psh. This guy," Joe said, disgusted. Paul always tried to bring everyone around him down. But the comment still stung. It was just a little too close to the truth.

"Joe, ignore him," Dez said. "Now let's fix you up. You going to keep that cat in your lap?"

"Is it okay that I do that?" 22 asked as Joe hopped down from her shoulders and settled into her lap.

"Suit yourself," Dez said, throwing an apron around her. "You're the boss."

"I am?" 22 looked surprised. And pleased.

"When you're in this chair, yeah, you are," Dez replied.

"So . . . can I have one of those?" 22 pointed to a cup full of lollipops.

"Sure, Joe." Dez handed one over.

She quickly unwrapped it and popped it into her mouth. "Cool. I like being in the chair," she said.

In her lap, Joe was slowly dying of embarrassment.

"Be cool! Get your head in the game!" he chided 22.

Dez fired up the clippers. 22 jumped at the sound. "Ah! Little chain saw!"

That did it. Joe stood up in her lap. "I need you to settle down!" he commanded. "If you keep this up, you're going to make things worse!"

Dez raised his eyebrows, looking down at the yelling cat. *Meow! Meow! Meow! Meow!*

"Look," he said to 22, "I can deal with some freaky stuff, but if this cat don't chill, we're going to have to put it outside."

22 smirked at Joe. "Well, what's it gonna be, kitty?"

"Meow," Joe grumbled.

"I'm sorry," 22 said to Dez. "Please continue."

Dez raised the clippers and began to cut, still shaking his head at the disaster. "Sometimes change is good, man," he said. "You've been rocking that same cut for a while."

"Well, Dez," 22 said, sucking on her lollipop, "for hundreds of years, I've had no style at all."

Paul burst out laughing. "You can say that again!"

22 glanced at him, confused. She didn't get the joke. "But then my life changed," she told Dez.

"Really? What happened?"

"Well," said 22, clearly enjoying the attention, "I was existing as a theoretical construct in a hypothetical way station between life and death."

Joe put his paws over his ears. If 22 was going to make him sound like a lunatic, he didn't want to hear it. He only hoped it would be over quickly.

But 22 was just getting started. Ten minutes later, she was still talking. "And by the time I got to mentor number two hundred sixty-six, I was seriously asking, like, what is all the fuss about?" she blathered. "Like, is all this living really worth dying for? You know what I mean?"

Silence. All the other conversations in the shop had ceased. Everyone was staring at 22.

Joe took his paws off his ears and covered his eyes. He didn't know which was worse—listening to 22, or watching everyone else listen to her.

"Wow, you're really in a sharing mood today, Joe," Dez said. "I . . . uh . . . never knew you had such an interesting education. I just thought you went to music school."

"And another thing . . . ," 22 prattled on, "they say you're born to do something, but how do you figure out what that thing is? And what if you pick up the wrong thing? Or somebody else's thing, you know? Then you're stuck!"

Dez chuckled. "I never planned on cutting heads for a living. But I wouldn't call myself stuck."

"But you were born to be a barber. Weren't you?" 22 asked. She darted a confused glance at Joe. After all, that was what he'd told her.

"I wanted to be a veterinarian," Dez replied. "I always loved animals."

Joe uncovered his eyes. A vet? That was Dez's dream? Dez had been cutting his hair for years. How had Joe never known?

"Why didn't you do that?" 22 asked.

"I was planning to. After I got out of the Navy," Dez explained. "And then my daughter got sick, and . . ." He shrugged. "Barber school is a lot cheaper than vet school."

"That's too bad you're stuck as a barber and now you're unhappy," 22 said.

"Whoa, slow your roll, there, Joe. I'm happy as a clam, my man. Not everyone can be Charles Drew, inventing blood transfusions."

"Or me, playing piano with Dorothea Williams," 22 added.

That set Paul off again. "Ha-ha," he guffawed. "You are not all that. Anyone could play in a band if they wanted to."

Joe resisted the urge to use Paul's leg as a scratching post. But 22 just looked confused. She didn't understand why Paul kept razzing her.

Then a light bulb seemed to go on in her head. "Oh, I get it. He's just criticizing me to cover up the pain of his own failed dreams."

The whole shop laughed.

Dang! Joe thought. *Razor-sharp comeback, 22!*

Paul gave Joe a wounded look. "You cut deep, Joe." He got up and headed for the door.

"I wonder why sitting in this chair makes me want to tell you things, Dez," 22 said.

"That's the magic of the chair," Dez replied. "That's why I love this job. I get to meet interesting folks like you. Make them happy." Dez put down his clippers and picked up a small hand mirror. "And make them handsome," he added, handing it to 22.

22 turned her head left, then right, admiring the new cut. "Wow! Am I crazy, or do I look younger?"

Dez smiled. He untied Joe's apron and shook the clippings onto the floor. "I may not have invented blood transfusions," he said, "but I am most definitely saving lives."

With Joe softly meowing instructions, 22 collected Joe's hat and coat and paid.

Dez walked them to the door. "I don't know about this crazy-cat-guy thing, man," Dez said, shaking 22's hand, "but it is nice to finally talk to you about something other than jazz, Joe."

"How come we never talked about that before?" 22 asked.

"You never asked," Dez replied. "But I'm glad you did this time."

The other customers waved Joe goodbye, wishing him luck at the show. They stepped out onto the street, 22 holding Joe in her arms.

Joe noticed she had a sly look on her face. She lifted her hand from her pocket to show him a fistful of lollipops.

"I grabbed a couple of road lollies," she told Joe.

She unwrapped one, popped it in her mouth, and walked off with a spring in her step.

Joe smiled to himself. *It's too bad she doesn't ever want to live on Earth,* he thought. *When it comes right down to it, 22 is a pretty good soul.*

Fourteen

At that moment, on the other side of the city, Terry the accountant was closing in.

In the hospital room Joe had escaped from just hours before, Terry slithered around, looking for clues. Her eyes darted this way and that, taking in the sink, the heart monitor, the bed. Terry's ability to change her two-dimensional outline form into simple lines allowed her to blend into almost anything.

She left the hospital and proceeded to explore the streets of New York, disappearing into the tangent lines of gates and sidewalks. Then she arrived at Joe's apartment. Terry slid around the room, rifled through his record collection, and looked at the framed photos on top of his piano.

Next, she exited the apartment and hid in a nearby

pedestrian signal. From there, she spotted Joe (who she didn't know was actually 22) exiting a barbershop. He had a cat on his shoulders. As she watched, Joe stopped to talk to a man coming out of a sandwich shop.

"Hey, Paul!" 22 hailed the man. "That was some fun smack talk!"

Paul looked at her suspiciously. "You know, thugs got feelings, too, Joe."

"You don't look thuggish to me," replied 22. "You seem like a nice guy who just needs some encouragement. Here, have a lollipop."

Paul took the sweet, looking surprised. "Well . . . thanks, man."

"And sorry about hurting your feelings," 22 added.

"It's good," Paul replied. "Next time I'll come correct."

As they went on talking, Terry slithered around the corner ahead. Then she set her trap.

Terry opened a portal like a manhole in the sidewalk and hid herself. When Joe walked around the corner, he would step into the portal. Then she'd have him!

Terry could hear 22 and Paul saying goodbye. "Come to Terry . . . ," she murmured.

Musician Joe Gardner is about to audition for the legendary Dorothea Williams Quartet. Playing with Dorothea would be a lifelong dream come true!

During his audition, Joe plays a piano solo for Dorothea. This is his chance to show her that he was born to play jazz.

Joe's fingers dance across the piano keys as he gets lost in the music. He pours his soul into the audition!

The band is impressed with Joe! Dorothea tells him to be at the club in time for their show that night.

Joe shares the good news: he's the newest member
of the Dorothea Williams Quartet!

Joe doesn't watch where he's walking
and falls into a manhole!

Joe wakes up in a mysterious place. He has also transformed into a translucent soul!

Joe meets a stubborn soul named 22. Unfortunately, she is his only hope of getting back to Earth.

Joe finally makes it back to Earth, but he ends up in
the body of a hospital therapy cat, Mr. Mittens!

22 is horrified when she ends up on Earth, too—
in the body of Joe!

Joe realizes that 22 is hungry.
A slice of New York pizza makes everything better!

Joe and 22 find Moonwind, a traveler from the Astral Plane.
Moonwind says he can get Joe back into his own body.

Connie, the best student in Joe's class, stops by for a lesson. She is a natural at the trombone!

Joe and 22 visit Buddy's Barbershop.
Joe needs to look good for tonight's show!

Libba, Joe's mother, owns and runs a tailor's shop.
She makes sure Joe looks sharp for the big gig.

Inside Joe's body, 22 discovers how wondrous
and magnificent life can be.

Footsteps moved toward her. One second later, a soul plunged into the darkness like a fish into a tank.

"GOTCHA!" Terry shouted, emerging from her hiding spot. "Thought you could cheat the universe? Well, you thought wrong. I'm the accountant, and I'm here to— Oops!"

Terry broke off. The soul trembling before her wasn't Joe—it was Paul!

"You're not Joe Gardner." Terry gave a nervous chuckle. "My mistake. We'll just get you right back into your body." Quickly, she spit Paul out of the portal.

An instant later, Paul's soul was back in his body. He stood there clutching his bag of potato chips and shaking like a leaf as Terry dusted him off.

"There you go. No harm, no foul," she said.

"M-m-m-m . . . ," Paul stammered.

Terry put an arm around Paul's shoulders. "Look, fella. I'm thinking there's no reason we can't keep this little incident between us, eh?"

Paul just stared at her, ashen-faced.

"Mistakes happen. And it's not your time. Unless you keep eating those processed foods, am I right?" Terry joked.

Seeing that it was probably time to go, Terry vanished.

Then a second later, she reappeared inside Paul's bag of chips. "But seriously, stay away from those processed foods," she told him sternly. She vanished again.

Paul screamed and threw the chips into a trash can.

Terry dusted off her hands. That was that. Now she could get back to finding Joe Gardner.

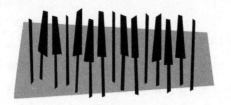

Fifteen

22 strolled down the sidewalk, enjoying her lollipop. Joe walked behind her so he could admire his new haircut. *22 is right,* he thought. *It really does make me look younger.*

"You know what? You did all right back there. How'd you know how to deal with Paul?" he asked her.

"I didn't," 22 said. "I just improvised. Hey, just like jazz! I was jazzing!"

"First of all," Joe said, "'jazzing' is not a word. And second, music and life operate by very different rules. . . ."

He trailed off, realizing that 22 was no longer behind him. She had stopped at a telephone pole covered in flyers.

"It says take one!" she said.

"Don't—" Joe began. But 22 was already joyfully ripping strips off the flyers. "Or do. Okay, fine," Joe said with a shrug. Who was he to ruin her fun?

22 jogged back to Joe, her hands full of little strips of paper. "'Man with a Van.' I got a few in case we need a lot of vans." She shoved them in her pocket.

"Uh-huh." Joe rolled his eyes. "Now let's get back to the plan. We go to The Half Note and wait there for Moonwind. It's around four p.m. right now. . . ."

Once again, 22 wasn't paying any attention. She'd stopped in front of a window to smile at her reflection. A moment later, she was running her hand along a fence, listening to the sound of it.

"Hey! I made a song! I'm jazzing!" she said.

"Enough of the jazzing," said Joe. "We need to get somewhere—"

"Woo-hoo!" 22 paused atop a subway grate, enjoying the blast of warm air. An instant later, she was lying on her belly on the grate, her arms out like Superman. "Hoo-hoo-hoo-hoo!"

Whoosh! The gust of air blew the hat off 22's head. It sailed down the street.

"I got it!" 22 jumped up and ran after the hat. But as she bent over to pick it up, Joe heard an awful ripping sound.

"Huh. You were right," 22 said, straightening up. "These pants *are* loosening."

Joe gasped in horror. He dashed over to inspect the damage. His pants had almost split in two! "Take off the jacket!" he ordered. "Tie it around your waist. Quickly!"

22 did as he asked. Joe paced the sidewalk.

"What do we do? I can't find a tailor now. . . ." As soon as the words left his mouth, Joe knew what he had to do. It was the only solution—and it filled him with dread.

"We're going have to go to Mom's," Joe told 22.

"Okay!" she said cheerily.

"You don't understand," Joe replied. "Mom doesn't know about this gig. And she's not going to like it."

22 frowned. "Okay."

"She's the only one who can fix this," Joe explained, as much for his own sake as 22's.

"Okay," said 22.

"Stop saying okay!" Joe snapped. "We've got to catch the subway. Come on." Striding ahead, Joe led the way toward the subway that would take them across town.

A few minutes later, they were heading down the steps into the station. 22 carried Joe in one arm. With the other hand, she munched on a bagel they'd picked up along the way.

Joe tried to think of how he was going to explain things to his mother. Libba was sharp. If they weren't careful, she would know something was up.

"My mom doesn't know about the gig, and I want to keep it that way, okay?" he warned 22.

22 nodded. "Right, because she thinks you're a failure."

"What?" Joe exclaimed.

"I didn't say that! *You* did. Up here." 22 tapped her head.

"Look, my mom has her own definition of success," Joe replied. "And being a professional musician isn't it. So, let's see . . ." Joe leaped down from 22's arms and began to pace. "I need the suit fixed for a school band recital."

He nodded. It seemed plausible. Joe figured Libba wouldn't mind helping if it was for his school job. It was a shame he had to lie, though.

"There's no reason she needs to know," Joe told himself. "All the times I've been so close to getting my dreams, something always gets in the way. You know what I mean, 22?"

But 22 wasn't next to him. She'd stopped to watch a musician on the subway platform. The man strummed his guitar, singing soulfully. As 22 listened, her body seemed to relax. She swayed to the music, her eyes full of wonder.

"I've heard music before," she said. "But I've never felt like this inside."

"Of course you love music now," Joe said. "Because you're *me*."

A little girl approached and dropped a few coins into the musician's cup. Seeing this, 22 broke off a piece of her bagel and dropped it into the cup, too. She caught up with Joe just as the subway train pulled into the station.

While the doors closed behind them, Joe found a seat. The train jolted forward, throwing 22 off-balance. At once, she turned it into a game. Spreading her feet wide, she pretended to surf the subway car.

"Ha-ha!" 22 flung her arms out, accidentally hitting another passenger.

"Hey! Take it easy!" the man snarled.

"I'm sorry!" 22 ducked her head. She scuttled over to sit down next to Joe.

"Don't worry about it," Joe told her. "The subway does that to some people."

"Does what?" 22 asked.

"It wears you down. It stinks. It's hot. It's crowded. And you have to take it every day to a job you don't like." Joe thought for a moment. "The subway is a perfect reminder of just how stuck in life you are. . . ."

He was answered by a loud slurp. Joe glanced over. 22 was sucking down a giant cup of soda.

"Where'd you get that?" Joe asked.

"Under the seat," 22 replied. "Can you believe it? Still half full—"

In reply, Joe slapped the cup out of her hands.

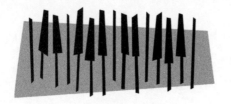

Sixteen

For all his careful plotting, Joe never got a chance to try out his lie. As they entered Libba's Tailor Shop, they saw Melba and Lulu, his mother's two employees. When they saw Joe, the women lit up with smiles.

"Joey, we heard the news!"

"I'm so proud of you, baby boy!"

Joe groaned inwardly. He knew the game was up. If Lulu and Melba knew about the gig, then Libba surely did, too.

From the back of the shop came the sound of Libba clearing her throat. At once, Lulu and Melba became serious.

"Your mama's in the back," Lulu said in a hushed voice.

They all looked toward Libba's office. "You've got to go in there," Joe told 22.

"I don't want to!" she exclaimed.

Joe prodded her with a paw. "You have to! We need this suit fixed!"

22 gulped and shuffled toward the back of the shop. As they passed Melba, the older woman smiled and tilted her cheek toward them.

"You forgetting something, Joey?" she asked, tapping it with a finger.

22 looked at her blankly.

"Kiss her," Joe whispered.

22 balked. "You're kidding."

"I always kiss Melba when I see her. Just do it," Joe ordered.

22 considered Melba for a moment. Then she grabbed her face and planted a huge kiss on her lips!

"No, no, no!" Joe hissed. "Not on the lips!"

Mortified, 22 released Melba and scurried toward the back of the shop. Melba didn't seem to mind, though.

"I'll take another kiss when you get back, Joey!" she called after them.

In the back room, they found Libba pinning a dress on a mannequin. Her back was to them, but Joe could tell by the way she stabbed the pins into the fabric that she was upset. "So much for being done chasing after gigs, huh?" she said coldly.

She turned and spotted the cat draped across her son's shoulders. Joe leaped onto a nearby dresser. "I hope that cat isn't supposed to be some kind of peace offering," Libba said.

"Just say you rescued it," Joe whispered to 22.

"Um, no. It's mine," 22 told Libba. "I rescued it."

"Hmm." Libba pursed her lips. "Too bad you can't rescue your career."

Joe felt a flare of anger. Libba really knew how to push his buttons. But he wasn't going to get into it with her today. He took a deep breath, trying to keep his cool. "Just ask her nicely if she can fix my suit," Joe told 22.

"So, Mom, is there any way you can fix this?" 22 asked Libba. She removed the suit jacket and showed Libba the tear.

"Whoa! I don't need to see that!" Libba said, wincing.

"I know." 22 grimaced. "Embarrassing, right? So you'll fix it?"

Libba folded her arms. "No."

"What?" Joe and 22 cried in unison. Joe couldn't

believe it. His own mama would let him play a gig at The Half Note with a rip the size of Manhattan in his pants?

"How long are you going to keep doing this, Joey?" Libba asked. "You tell me you're going to accept the full-time position. Then instead I hear you've taken on another gig."

"Tell her that this one's different!" Joe hissed to 22.

"This one's different!" 22 repeated.

Libba's face hardened. Joe knew what was coming. They'd been here a million times before.

"Does this 'gig' have a pension? Health insurance?" she demanded. Joe knew the lecture so well, he could mouth the words along with her. "No? Then it's the same as the other ones."

"Come on," Joe said angrily to 22. He should have known better than to come here. "We'll get a suit off the rack somewhere." He hopped off the dresser, heading for the door. "My mom has never understood what I'm trying to do with my life."

"My mom has never understood what I'm trying to do with my life," 22 repeated.

Joe froze. So did Libba. "What did you just say?" she demanded.

Right away, 22 seemed to grasp the enormity of her error. "Can I run away now, like you usually do?" she whispered to Joe.

Joe considered. He *did* feel like running away. But what good would that do? It was all out in the open now. If he didn't take this chance to say what was in his heart, he never would.

Joe leaped back into 22's arms. "Not this time," he told her. "Repeat after me."

22 did as he asked. For the first time since the wrong soul had landed in Joe's body, the words coming out of his mouth belonged to Joe.

"Mom, I know we've had some rough times. But you're right. I can't be truthful with you. Because no matter what I do, you disapprove."

Libba looked taken aback. Her son had never spoken to her that way before. "Look, I know you love playing . . . ," she began.

"Then how come except for at church, you seem happiest when I don't?" Joe interrupted. "I finally land the gig of my life, and you're upset!"

"You didn't see how tough being a musician was on your father," Libba replied, her voice rising. "I don't want to see you struggle like that!"

"So Dad could pursue his dreams, but I can't?" Joe demanded.

"Your father had me," Libba reminded him. "Most of the time, this shop was what paid the bills. So when I'm gone, who's going to pay yours?"

"Music is all I think about," Joe told her. "From the moment I wake up in the morning to the moment I fall asleep at night."

"You can't eat dreams for breakfast, Joey," Libba said sadly.

"Then I don't want to eat if I don't have my music!" Joe exclaimed. "This isn't about a career. It's my reason for living! And I know Dad would have felt the same way."

Joe paused. He was breathing hard. But he'd come this far. He needed to tell her the whole truth. "I'm afraid that if I died today, my life would have amounted to nothing," he admitted.

Libba's eyes moistened. She stared at her son as if seeing him for the first time. "Joey. You never told me that before."

I tried, Mom, Joe thought. *I've been trying to tell you that my whole life.*

"You're just like your dad," she said, her voice full of tenderness. "You have a musician's heart." Libba looked at Joe for a long moment. Then she went to a cabinet and pulled out a large box. "Let's make this work instead," she said, lifting the lid.

Joe gasped. It was his father's best suit—a beautiful blue wool gabardine. Libba had made it herself. Joe had seen his dad play dozens of shows in it.

"Lulu! Melba!" Libba called into the other room. "Bring your good scissors in here. We got work to do!"

Half an hour later, 22 stood before the full-length mirror while Libba, Lulu, and Melba surrounded him, making the final adjustments. In his cat body, Joe watched from the top of the dresser. With his sharp new haircut and the elegant suit, Joe thought he'd never looked better.

"That is one fine wool suit, if I do say so myself," Libba said.

22 was clearly enjoying herself, too. "Can I try that on?" she asked, pointing to a silk handkerchief.

"Of course you can." Libba helped her tuck a pale blue handkerchief into the suit's breast pocket.

"Thank you . . . um, Mom." 22 hugged her.

Libba's arms tightened around her son. "Ray would have been so proud of you, baby," she murmured. "Like I've always been."

She pulled back and gave 22 a stern look. "You heard me, right? That's a wool suit, not polyester. So don't go putting that cat on your shoulders again!"

"Yes, ma'am," 22 and Joe chorused.

Libba walked them to the door of the shop. Out on the street, Joe looked back. He could see Libba still standing in the doorway, watching them go.

"Thanks, Mom," he said quietly.

22 started off, and Joe ran to catch up with her. "Wow, that was amazing!" he said. "Know what that felt like? That felt like jazz!"

"Yeah, you were jazzing!" said 22.

Joe laughed. "Okay," he agreed. "Jazzing."

Seventeen

Joe and 22 caught the downtown train and made it to The Half Note with minutes to spare. For the first time since his soul had left his body, Joe knew everything was going to be all right.

"We made it!" he exclaimed as they hurried up to the club. "Moonwind's going to be here any minute. This is going to work!"

22 stopped under the marquee, and Joe caught his breath. *There I am,* he thought. *The Half Note. I really did it.* He knew he'd remember this moment for the rest of his life.

"I can't believe how good I look! The suit . . . the cut. Just look at me! Turn just a little," he told 22. Joe wanted to admire himself from all angles.

"Like this?" 22 put her hands on her hips, looking

back at Joe over her shoulder. Joe laughed as she struck pose after pose. "Right? I wear you well, Joe."

As their laughter faded, they sat down on the curb to wait for Moonwind.

It was a beautiful fall afternoon. An old man passed on the sidewalk, holding the hand of his skipping granddaughter. At a sidewalk café down the street, people chatted over cups of coffee.

22 turned her face to the sunlight. As she did, a breeze blew through the branches of a maple tree. Dozens of seedpods whirled down toward her, spinning like tiny helicopters.

22 caught one in her palm. She gazed at it thoughtfully. "Hey, Joe?"

"Yeah?"

22 took a deep breath. "I'm ready."

"Me too," said Joe. "Don't worry. Moonwind will be here any second."

"No, I'm ready to come here," 22 explained. "I want to get my Earth Pass."

"Really?" Joe said, startled. "What changed your mind?"

22 gazed out at the world around them. "I always

110

said Earth was dumb. But I never tasted it. Or breathed it. I never knew what it meant to be warm. Or to feel the breeze. Or to have a friend. Turns out, life is incredible! Just look what I found!"

She began to remove objects from her suit pocket. "You mom sewed your suit from this cute spool," she said, holding up a spool of thread. "When I was nervous, Dez gave me this." She took out a lollipop, then a piece of bagel, cradling them like treasures. "A guy on the subway yelled at me—it was scary, but I kind of liked that, too. Then I saw this other guy singing, and it was the most beautiful thing I'd ever heard. So, do you think I'm ready?" 22 asked Joe earnestly. "Maybe sky-watching can be my Spark. Or walking. I'm really good at walking."

"Those aren't Sparks, 22," he explained. "That's just everyday living. But hey, when you get back to the You Seminar, you can give it an honest try."

At the mention of the You Seminar, the hope seemed to drain from 22's face. "Joe, I've been at the You Seminar for hundreds of years. And I've never felt this close."

"Joe!" someone shouted. Joe turned at the sound

of his name. Moonwind ran toward them. His arms were full of bongos, crystals, and other mystical paraphernalia.

"Who's ready to go home?" Moonwind exclaimed, plunking his load down on the sidewalk. "The stars are almost in alignment! Come, sit! I'll have you back in your body in no time!"

"All right!" said Joe.

"No," 22 said.

They turned to her in surprise.

"I've got to find it here. On Earth," 22 explained. "This is my only chance to find my Spark!"

"Sorry, there's no time," Joe said firmly. "I need to get my body back. Now." He walked over to Moonwind.

22's expression hardened. "No," she said again, louder. "I'm the boss. I'm in the chair."

Before Joe could say another word, she sprinted away.

"22!" he cried desperately, tearing after her. "You come back here!"

"Leave me alone!" she hollered, oblivious to the concerned glances of other people on the street. "I'm trying to find my purpose!"

She turned a corner and disappeared into a crowd.

Joe dodged through feet and legs until he spotted her again. She was heading for the subway entrance. Joe sprinted toward it as fast as his cat legs would take him.

In the station, 22 hopped the turnstile and headed for the platform. Joe streaked after her. "You stole my body!" he yelled.

22 shoved through the crowd of commuters, and kept on going. She turned into an empty corridor, with Joe on her tail. He was gaining on her. He could see the exit sign up ahead, and 22's feet pounding toward it.

Joe put on a burst of speed, his claws gripping at the tile floor. He couldn't let 22 reach the exit—

And then, suddenly, Joe and 22 were suspended in darkness. It was as if they'd stepped through a doorway—one second they were racing through the subway station, the next they were floating in empty black space. They'd fallen right into Terry's trap.

Joe's soul floated out of his cat body. 22's soul floated out of Joe's body. Looking down, Joe could see himself lying below on the subway platform. He stretched his arms out toward his body, but he was being pulled in the opposite direction.

"It's your time to go, Joe Gardner," Terry said, appearing next to him. A portal opened above Joe. On the other side, he could see the Soul World.

"No, no, no!" Joe resisted with all his might. He propelled himself downward through the black space toward his body. Just a few more inches . . .

"Oh, no, you don't!" Terry growled.

With a great force, she swept Joe upward. The moment he flew through the portal, Terry snapped it shut.

Eighteen

Joe looked around. The grimy subway station was gone. All around him, he saw gentle blue-green rolling hills and gossamer buildings.

He was back at the You Seminar. 22 stood next to him. Her arms were folded across her chest. She glared at Joe like a sullen teenager.

"No, no, no!" Joe wailed. "I was going to play with Dorothea Williams!"

"And I was going to find my Spark! But you wouldn't even give me five minutes," 22 shot back.

"I had a purpose!" Joe exclaimed. "My life was finally going to change! I lost everything because of you!"

"Joe!" a voice interrupted sternly.

Joe turned. Terry was watching them.

"You cheated," she told Joe.

That stopped Joe cold. She was right. He'd tried to cheat death. And he had lost.

Terry opened a portal. Through the window, Joe could see the humming white light of The Great Beyond. "Come on, Mr. Gardner. It's time," she said.

As Joe stepped toward the portal, he heard cheers behind him. A group of Jerrys were gathered around 22. They were all patting her on the back, congratulating her.

"Well, I'll be!"

"22 got an Earth Pass?"

"This is incredible!"

Joe could hardly believe his eyes. 22's Personality Profile had changed into an Earth Pass.

22 seemed just as surprised as he was. She stared down at it with a bewildered expression.

The counselors turned to Joe. "22 completed the program!" one said. "So wonderful. And after all these years. I never thought this day would come."

"I knew you could do it, 22. Just needed the right mentor, I guess! Right, Joe?" said another counselor, smiling at him.

"But what filled in the last box?" 22 asked, looking confused.

The counselors didn't seem to hear her. They were too busy congratulating Joe. "Great work, Mr. Gardner!" they said over and over.

One of the Jerrys ushered 22 toward the Earth Portal. "Let's get you in line," she said.

"She only got that badge because she was in *my* body," Joe grumbled. Resigned, he turned back to the portal to The Great Beyond.

"Wait!" said 22. "I want Joe to take me."

"Of course," the counselor said smoothly. He waved Joe over. "Go ahead."

Terry scowled. "Now, wait just a minute—"

She moved forward as if to stop Joe. But the counselors blocked her path.

"Terry, you've done a super job."

"We'll take it from here."

"You're amazing."

"Well, thank you," the accountant said, mollified. She did a little victory dance. "Terrytime!"

Together, Joe and 22 walked to the Earth Portal. An awkward silence stretched between them.

When they reached the edge of the platform, 22 suddenly turned and thrust her Earth Pass at him. "Take it," she whispered.

"What?" Joe said, startled.

"Take it, and go back to your life," 22 told him.

"But why?"

"It filled in because I was in your body, being you," 22 explained. "It's *your* Spark that changed it, not mine." She pressed the pass into Joe's hands.

Joe didn't know what to say. "22 . . . I . . . ," he started.

"I don't have a purpose, okay? I'm broken," 22 said. She glanced over her shoulder. "You'd better hurry. Before Jerry comes back. Go!"

She turned and disappeared into the crowd of new souls.

Joe looked down at the pass in his hands. This was what he'd wanted all along. So why did it feel so wrong?

"I have to ask . . . ," a voice said next to him.

Joe jumped, startled as a counselor appeared. Quickly, he hid the Earth Pass behind his back.

The counselor peered down at him. "How the dickens did you do it? Get the Personality Profile to change?"

"Oh, uh, I—I . . . ," Joe stammered. "I just let her walk a mile in my shoes, you could say."

"Well, it worked. I know it's hard," the counselor added, misunderstanding Joe's unhappy expression. "You should probably get going to The Great Beyond." The counselor turned to leave.

"Hey," Joe said, "we never found out what 22's purpose was."

Jerry turned back. "Excuse me?"

"The Spark," Joe said. "Was it music? Biology? Walking?"

"We don't assign purposes," the counselor replied. "Where did you get that idea?"

"Because I have piano!" Joe said. "It's what I was born to do. That's my Spark."

"A Spark isn't a soul's purpose." The counselor shook his head in amusement. "Oh, you mentors and your passions! Your purposes! Your meanings of life! So basic." He walked away, chuckling to himself.

Joe stared after him, unsettled. What was he saying? Was he saying passions didn't matter? And if they didn't, then what was Joe's Spark?

"No! My Spark is music. I know it is!" he exclaimed angrily. Placing the pass around his neck, Joe leaped down to Earth to prove it.

Nineteen

Joe woke up in his own body with a sea of anxious faces staring down at him. Above them, he could see the fluorescent lights of the subway corridor.

Joe sat up. He looked at his hands. They were brown-skinned, long-fingered, strong—his very own beautiful hands. He was back in his body!

Quickly, Joe checked his watch. It was five minutes to seven. He still had time to make it to The Half Note!

Joe jumped to his feet. Pushing through the crowd of onlookers, he sprinted for the exit.

Joe arrived at The Half Note at one minute after seven o'clock. As soon as he entered the club, he saw Curley.

"Mr. G?" the drummer said in surprise.

"Curley, I made it! I'm ready to go!" Joe said breathlessly.

"You're too late, man," Curley said, shaking his head.

"Let me talk to Dorothea."

"No, man. She don't play that!" Curley held up his hands to stop him. But Joe pushed past him. He found Dorothea's dressing room and barged through the door.

Dorothea was sitting at her dressing table, getting ready for the show. "Who let this lunatic in here?" she snapped.

"You've got to give me another chance!" Joe exclaimed.

"This is my band. I decide who plays," she told Joe coldly.

"If you don't go with me, you'll be making the biggest mistake of your career," Joe shot back.

Dorothea turned toward him and stood up. "Oh, yeah? Why is that?"

"My only purpose on this planet is to play," he told Dorothea. "It's what I was meant to do. And nothing's going to stop me."

Dorothea stared daggers at him. Joe held her gaze.

Then, to his amazement, she smiled. "Well, aren't you an arrogant one?" she said. "I guess you really are a jazz player." As she passed Joe, she gave a tiny nod of approval. "Nice suit."

Dorothea brushed past Curley, who was standing in the doorway, watching the whole scene. Curley grinned and gave Joe a double thumbs-up. Joe was back in the band!

As soon as he was alone, Joe slumped against the dressing table, sighing with relief. He'd done it. Despite everything, he'd made his dream come true.

Joe's eyes met his reflection. He straightened up and fixed his tie.

"Get ready, Joe Gardner," he said, smiling. "Your life is about to start."

Twenty

That night at The Half Note, Joe played as he never had before. He set fire to the piano with his fingers. He put his soul into every chord.

Joe wasn't the only one in the Zone that night. They were all on top of their game. The quartet gelled like they'd been playing together for years, not just a single afternoon. It was all Joe had hoped for, the gig of his life.

And then it was over.

The lights came up, and the band stood to take their bows. Joe was slick with sweat, breathing like he'd run a mile. The whole audience was on their feet, applauding wildly. He could see Libba, Melba, and Lulu cheering for him.

He glanced over at Dorothea. When she caught his eye, she smiled and nodded.

"Welcome to the quartet, Teach," she said.

Joe could have stayed in that moment forever. But too soon, it was time to go home. After the audience had left, the other musicians packed up their instruments and headed for the door.

"Nice work! That was killer!" Curley said, slapping Joe on the back.

"Yeah, that was amazing." Joe laughed. He was still on cloud nine.

Curley and Miho, the bassist, waved their goodbyes and headed off. Joe turned to his mother, Lulu, and Melba, who had stayed to see him out.

"You've done us proud. Yes, you have," said Lulu, pinching Joe's cheeks.

Libba wrapped him in a hug. "I'm so proud of you, Joey!" With one last squeeze, she let Joe go and headed for the curb, where Melba and Lulu were already getting into a cab. "Got to get to bed!" she called to her son. "We old!"

Joe waved. But as the cab pulled away, he felt his elation fading.

Just then, Dorothea came out of the club. She walked over to Joe. For a moment, they stood side by side, looking out at the quiet street.

"You play one hundred shows, and one of them is killer," Dorothea said. "You don't get many like tonight."

"Yeah, that was amazing. So now what happens?" Joe asked, trying to hold on to the excitement.

"We come back tomorrow night and do it all again," Dorothea said.

That was it? Joe said nothing.

But Dorothea must have seen something in his face, because she asked, "What's wrong, Teach?"

"It's just . . ." Joe struggled to find the words. "I've been waiting on this day my entire life. I thought I'd feel . . . different."

"Mm." Dorothea gave him one of her inscrutable looks. After a moment, she said, "A fish swims up to an older fish and says, 'I'm trying to find the ocean.' 'The ocean?' says the older fish. 'That's what you're in right now. 'This?' says the young fish. 'This is water. What I want is the *ocean*.'"

Dorothea flagged down a cab. "See you tomorrow," she told Joe. She stepped in and closed the door.

Joe watched her pull away, feeling confused. He began walking toward the subway.

On the long ride home, Joe gazed at his reflection in the darkened window. By the time Joe reached his stop, it was very late and snow had started to fall. He headed down the same path he'd taken hundreds of times before.

Joe let himself into his apartment and walked over to the piano. As he sat down on the bench, he felt a lump in his jacket. He reached into the pocket and pulled out a handful of junk—a pizza crust, part of a bagel, a lollipop, a spool of thread, a winged seedpod. All the things 22 had collected during their day together.

Joe dropped the pile on a side table. He absentmindedly began to play.

As his fingers ran over the keys, his gaze fell on the seedpod. He had a sudden, clear memory of looking up toward the tree as dozens of seedpods spiraled down toward him. It had been a beautiful moment.

And the pizza crust . . . Joe had a flash of 22 gobbling a pizza slice with pure joy.

Joe picked up the objects and carefully spread them out on the ledge of the piano. Then he began to play again, putting music to each memory that awoke within him.

The bagel crust reminded him of the soul singer in the subway, the moment 22 had learned to love music. He thought of 22 playing her own "music" on the fence, running a hand along the bars, and how excited she'd been to create something.

That made him think of Connie playing her heart out on her trombone. And then Dez in his barbershop, "saving lives" in his own way. And Libba snipping a thread on his father's suit . . .

Like a thread unspooling, moments of Joe's life came back to him, one after the other. The feel of Libba's gentle hands bathing him when he was small. The scratch of the record needle as he lay on the rug, listening to music with his parents. His first trip to the jazz club with his father, and the way the music had swelled inside him like a wave.

Other images flooded his mind. Riding a bike. Eating pie. Conducting the school band. Teaching Curley to play drums. Watching a baseball game from a rooftop. The feel of ocean waves on his toes.

This, Joe thought. *This is my life. All the single, precious moments.* It wasn't sad or wasted. It was beautiful.

And then he recalled 22 sitting under the tree outside The Half Note, her hopeful voice as she'd said, *Maybe sky-watching could be my Spark. Or walking.*

Those aren't Sparks, Joe had told her. *That's just regular living.*

But he'd had it wrong. All the small moments, the tiny joys—those were the things that made life worth living.

A wave of guilt washed over him. 22 had wanted to have a life. And he'd denied her the chance. He had to tell her that she really did have the Spark of life—it was her will to live life itself!

As Joe stared at the seedpod, he suddenly knew what he had to do. Closing his eyes, he began to play.

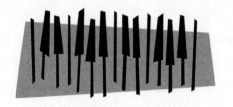

Twenty-One

Joe opened his eyes. He was back in the Zone. Overhead, he saw the swirling purples and blues of the Astral Plane sky. Someone was calling his name.

"Joe? Joe! Wake up!" said a familiar voice.

Joe sat up. He was sitting in the middle of a circle that had been drawn in the glittering black sand. Moonwind crouched next to him, looking concerned.

"Good heavens, man!" the mystic exclaimed. "Where did you run off to?"

"Moonwind!" Joe cried in relief. "I need your help. I messed up. Can you take me to 22?"

Moonwind's expression darkened. "Come on," he said, pulling Joe to his feet and leading him toward the ship. "I'll explain on the way."

As they sailed across the astral sands, Moonwind

told Joe what had happened while he'd been gone. After leaving Joe, 22 had returned to the Astral Plane. But she was different. She wouldn't talk to Moonwind, and when he'd called out to her, she'd run away. Dark astral dust now clung to her, and there was a hole in her chest where her Earth Pass should have been.

The ship slowed. In the distance, Joe could see a herd of lost souls moving across the sands.

Why did we stop here? Joe wondered. *Where is 22?*

Moonwind pulled out a telescope and handed it to Joe. Joe peered through the lens, wondering what he was supposed to be looking at. Suddenly, a blackened creature staggered into view. Like the other lost souls, its body was covered in black astral dust. But its cute chubby cheeks and buckteeth looked familiar to Joe. . . .

He gasped. "22's becoming a lost soul!"

How had it happened? What had made 22 so obsessed that she became like *this*?

"Get me closer!" Joe cried to Moonwind.

As the boat plunged forward, Joe called out to 22.

When 22 saw Moonwind's ship, she hissed like a furious cat, then bolted away.

Moonwind unfurled the tie-dyed sails, and they

raced after her. Joe readied the net gun. If they could just bring 22 in, he was sure they'd be able to help her.

Closer . . . , Joe urged silently. *Closer . . .*

As soon as 22 was in range, Joe fired the net. It wrapped around 22. But rather than slowing, 22 dived into the black astral sand and burrowed down.

The rope winch spun out like a fishing reel as she plowed deeper. Like a whale on a hook, she dragged the boat along with her.

SNAP! The rope came to its end and the whole ship plunged beneath the sand. Joe and Moonwind leaped off at the last second. They watched the ship sink under.

Joe thought all was lost. But a moment later, 22 popped up in the distance and took off running.

"22!" Joe cried, chasing after her.

At last, he managed to corner her among some astral rocks. She paced like a caged tiger, glaring at Joe.

"It's me, Joe." He stepped slowly closer, trying to keep his voice calm. "Easy, 22, easy. I just came back to give you this." Joe held up his Earth Pass.

At the sight of it, 22 hissed ferociously. She squeezed through a hole Joe hadn't noticed and disappeared.

Joe followed. He came out in a small room. At

once, Joe knew he was in 22's secret clubhouse. He recognized the name tags of all her mentors lining the walls.

But 22 didn't stop. She tore through the clubhouse and out into the You Seminar with Joe in pursuit.

At the You Seminar, Terry the accountant was receiving an award for her work in bringing Joe back. The other counselors watched as one of the Jerrys handed her a medal. "For correcting our absentminded mistakes and setting the count right, we are awarding you, Terry, with this trophy. As you requested," he added sarcastically.

Beaming, Terry stepped up to the podium to deliver her acceptance speech. "I am happy to accept this very special award that I requested, but which I absolutely deserve."

WHAM! 22 plowed through the ceremony, knocking over the podium and scattering the counselors. Joe chased after her.

"Joe Gardner?" Jerry said when she saw him.

The other Jerry turned and removed the medal from around Terry's neck. "And I'll just take that back."

22 ran dizzying circles through the You Seminar,

terrorizing the new souls. Joe tried again to catch her. But she was moving so fast, she was almost a blur.

Terry zipped underground and came up in front of 22, blocking her path. With a hiss, 22 snatched up the accountant. She tied Terry into a knot, then dashed away again.

Joe chased her all the way to the Earth Portal. 22 skidded to a stop at the edge of the platform. She teetered there, hissing with fear. She was trapped!

Joe inched slowly closer, blocking her escape. "I was wrong about life, 22. Please, will you listen?" He held out the Earth Pass again. "You *are* ready to live."

22 stopped hissing. She gave Joe such a look of understanding that for a second he thought he'd finally gotten through to her.

Then she opened her mouth . . . and swallowed him whole.

Twenty-Two

Joe found himself once again in darkness. Straining his eyes, he saw a small shape huddled in the near distance. It was 22.

Joe tried to go to her. But when he took a step, she moved farther away.

Joe followed, walking into a dark version of 22's clubhouse. It was filled with discarded Earth objects. Suddenly, strange apparitions floated out of the darkness, blocking his path. 22's voice echoed all around him:

"Not good enough. Nope. What's the point. Stupid. I can't, not good enough, no point, nothing, I just need to fill that last box. I give up."

Joe gasped as a phantom of Abraham Lincoln rose before him. But it wasn't Abe Lincoln from the history books. It was a monstrous Abe Lincoln, hollow-eyed and venomous. It added its voice to the barrage of angry words echoing around them. "You are dishonest! All you make are bad decisions! You are unwise, and you won't make it in the world! I don't want to be your mentor anymore!"

The horrifying Lincoln was joined by the phantom of Mother Teresa. "You're so selfish! No one would ever want to be around you!"

The famous psychiatrist Carl Jung appeared, to add his judgment as well. "You're a nitwit! Mentally unfit! An imbecile!"

More awful specters floated into the darkness. They were 22's former mentors, all back to haunt her. But they were deformed. Their words had been twisted in her mind.

Then, to Joe's horror, he saw a phantom of himself rise, larger than all the others.

"Those aren't purposes, YOU IDIOT!" roared the nightmare Joe. "That's just regular old living. You don't have a Spark because there's NOTHING you're good at! You only got that badge because you were in my body. You ruin everything. YOU. HAVE. NO. PURPOSE!"

Suddenly, nightmare Joe spewed black dust from

its mouth, creating a windstorm. Joe was pushed away and the Earth Pass was knocked out of his hands.

"No, no, no, no!" yelled Joe.

As he dug through the astral sands on the ground, frantically looking for the Earth Pass, he spotted something—it was the seedpod. He fought through the windstorm and finally reached 22. He placed the seedpod in her hand.

22 opened her eyes. As she looked down at the seedpod, the storm around them calmed. All at once, the darkness melted away. They were back at the edge of the Earth Portal, surrounded by counselors. 22 had returned to her regular form, and Joe was holding her in his arms.

"Joe?" 22 said, blinking at him in surprise. "What are you doing here?"

"I've got something for you," Joe replied. He placed the Earth Pass around 22's neck.

22 looked stunned. "But, Joe, this means you won't get to—"

Joe cut her off. "It's okay. I already did." He grinned. "Turns out, it was pretty great."

22 fingered the Earth Pass. "But . . . I never found my Spark," she said.

"I'd say that you're really great at jazzing," said Joe.

22 hesitated. She peeked over the edge of the platform at Earth far below. "I'm scared, Joe."

"I'll go with you," Joe assured her.

"You know you can't do that."

"I know." Joe nodded. "But I'll go as far as I can."

He glanced up at the counselors to make sure. They nodded their approval.

"Relax—I've done this before," Joe said. He took 22's hand in his. Together, they stepped off the edge.

As they fell down through space, the Earth, so tiny at first, seemed to grow bigger and bigger. Joe had never been skydiving, but he imagined it felt something like this.

This was less scary, though. After all, there was no chance he would ever land.

22 clung tightly to Joe's hand. Her eyes were squeezed shut.

"Hey! Take a look!" Joe said.

22 slowly opened one eye, then the other. She gasped in wonder.

As the Earth rose to meet them, Joe thought it had never looked so beautiful. They were close enough to see the swirling white patterns of the clouds. The golden gleam of sunlight on the oceans. The ripples of mountain peaks.

They fell in silence, admiring the view.

At some point, Joe felt himself slowing down. 22's Earth Pass started to glow. It was pulling her away from him.

Joe gave 22's hand one last squeeze. Then he let go.

He watched 22 fall to her new life. She grew smaller and smaller until she disappeared.

Joe's heart felt full. His only regret was that he wouldn't get to see 22's life on Earth. He wondered what it would be like.

Whatever happens, he thought, *it's going to be amazing.*

Twenty-Three

Joe stood on the slidewalk as it carried him toward The Great Beyond. Gazing up at the white light, he discovered that he no longer felt frightened. Its low hum seemed almost comforting.

But then again, Joe mused, what did he have to be afraid of? After all, he'd had a good life.

A *great* one.

"Mr. Gardner?" said a voice behind him.

He turned. To his surprise, he saw a counselor, the same one he'd met on his first trip to the You Seminar. She was holding a clipboard and smiling.

"Can I speak to you for a moment?" the counselor asked.

Joe walked over to her.

"I think I'm speaking for all the Jerrys when I say thank you," she said.

"For what?" Joe asked, confused.

"We're in the business of inspiration, Joe," the counselor replied. "But it's not often that we find ourselves inspired. So we all decided to get you a going-away gift." Jerry opened a window in the starry darkness around them. Through the portal, Joe saw the familiar blue-green marble of Earth.

"Hopefully you'll watch where you walk from now on," the counselor said kindly.

Joe smiled. "But what about Terry?" he asked.

"We worked it out with Terry," Jerry said vaguely. From the look on her face, Joe got the feeling that Terry didn't exactly know about the arrangement. But Joe wasn't going to ask too many questions.

"Thanks," said Joe as he stepped toward the open portal.

"Enjoy it," said Jerry.

"I will," replied Joe.

Back in New York, Joe walked out of his apartment building and onto the sidewalk. He closed his eyes, took a deep breath, and smiled.